HEART OF THE WITCH

WITCHES OF KEATING HOLLOW, BOOK 2

DEANNA CHASE

ABOUT THIS BOOK

Welcome to Keating Hollow, the enchanted village where love, cupcakes, and magic collide.

There are only three things that were ever important to Noel Townsend—love, family, and magic. Two out of three aren't bad. She's blessed with a large close-knit family and her magic has never been stronger. But love? That ended three years ago when her husband walked out on her and her daughter and never looked back.

These days Noel only has room in her pieced-together heart for her six-year old daughter. But when Drew Baker shows up on the doorstep of her inn with news of her husband, fate has other plans. And so does Drew. If he can get past her defenses, Drew is going to do everything in his power to heal the heart of a witch.

CHAPTER 1

DREW BAKER STROLLED down Main Street of Keating Hollow. As the Deputy Sheriff, he made it a point to remain visible, to connect with the citizens and business owners on a daily basis. There was no better way to deter crime than by keeping the lines of communication open.

Not that Keating Hollow was a hotbed of crime. Far from it. He'd just like to make sure it stayed that way.

"Officer Baker, hello," a familiar female voice called from behind him.

He suppressed a grimace and tried to keep his expression neutral as he turned around. "Good afternoon, Shannon. How's business?"

"Good. A Spoonful of Magic is keeping Miss Maple and me busy this holiday season." The pretty redhead moved closer to Drew and slid her hand up his arm. He stiffened as she added, "I was hoping you'd have time to help me taste test the new cinnamon hot cocoa."

He cleared his throat and took a step back as he patted his

stomach. "I'm trying to lay off the sweets this season. Probably not a good idea."

Her gaze traveled down to his flat abs. Raising one skeptical eyebrow, she said, "You're not that vain, are you, Drew? You wouldn't be making an excuse to get out of another date with me, now would you?"

His neck warmed as he shook his head. "I'm just really busy these days, Shannon. I wouldn't want a pretty girl like you waiting around for me."

She scoffed and opened her mouth to no doubt challenge his weak claim that he was too busy to date when another female called out from behind him, "Deputy Baker. There you are."

Drew turned and spotted Noel Townsend, the woman who ran the local inn. She looked different than usual. Hadn't she been a redhead just a few days ago? It appeared she'd dyed her hair blond. And to be honest, it suited her. She'd been beautiful before, but now she was elegant. "Something wrong, Noel?"

"No, no. Nothing's wrong," she said with a hint of a smile. "But I was hoping to talk to you about the town's security so we can be ready for the New Year's Day festival."

"Security?" Shannon asked, wrinkling her perfect little nose. "Since when does Keating Hollow need security? It's a town of witches."

Drew frowned, not at all sure what Noel was going on about. No one had said anything to him about needing security for the New Year's Day festival.

Noel tilted her head to the side and stared at Shannon, her brow furrowed. "Didn't you know new protection spells are cast every year?"

"Protection spells?" Shannon parroted, adjusting her glasses while confusion flashed in her whiskey-colored eyes.

2

Drew opened his mouth to ask what Noel was talking about, but she beat him to the punch.

"Don't worry about it, Shannon," Noel said as she slipped her arm through Drew's and patted his shoulder. "Officer Baker has it all under control." Noel glanced up at him, flashing him a secret mischievous smile. "Right, Drew?"

"Um, yes?" he said, finally catching on and feeling like an idiot for being two steps behind her in the conversation.

"You don't sound so sure," Shannon said, narrowing her eyes at him.

"He probably just needs my help finalizing the last of the spells," Noel said cheerfully. "I have time now." She glanced up at him, giving him a pointed look. "We can go back to the inn, and I can make some tea while we work out the details."

"Sure. Now's good," he said, relieved to be making his escape from Shannon. She was a nice woman, but she was a little too aggressive for his tastes.

Once they were halfway down the block and Shannon had slipped back into A Spoonful of Magic, he leaned down to Noel and said, "Thanks for that."

She pulled her arm out of his and shoved her hands into her pockets. "No problem. You looked a little like a deer in the headlights when she cornered you. I thought you could use a little help."

He winced. "Was it that obvious?"

She shrugged. "Probably not, at least not to someone who doesn't know you as well as I do."

The words hung in the air for just a moment as he remembered the summer right after he'd graduated when they'd both worked as camp counselors. The summer after his heart had cracked in two, and Noel Townsend had somehow managed to help piece it back together.

"Anyway," she said, breaking into his memory, "about that

security for the New Year's Day festival. That wasn't just an excuse to help you get away from Shannon, though you're welcome. I was thinking it might be a good idea to get prepared since Pansy Parker wrote that article about the event that went viral in the paranormal community a few weeks ago. The inn is completely booked and so are all the surrounding hotels up and down the coast."

"Seriously?" he asked, interested now. While Keating Hollow got its share of visitors, it was never *that* busy. It was a small Northern California town pretty far off the beaten path. "We should probably get some sort of head count."

She pushed the door of her inn open, and he followed her inside. "I have some numbers right here," she said, slipping behind the front desk.

He pulled his hat off and waited, admiring the graceful line of her neck as she tucked a lock of her blond hair behind her ear. There was no denying that Noel Townsend was a beautiful woman. She was long and lean, lithe like a model, only not as tall. She was about half a foot shorter than him, making her somewhere around five foot six. But it was her soulful blue eyes that usually captivated him, and the intensity there that stared back at him.

"Here we go," she said, handing him a Post It note without breaking eye contact. "Looks like about a thousand outsiders are planning to descend on us."

He rubbed a hand over the back of his neck and glanced away, suddenly uncomfortable with her unflinching gaze. "Looks like I'm going to need to call in some temporary help."

"Seems like a good idea. I've also got some spells ready to go that should help with surveillance."

He glanced down at her again and raised one eyebrow. "You do?"

Noel placed both hands on the counter and leaned forward.

Her sweater stretched across her chest, making it impossible for him to concentrate. "They're detection spells, and they make it easier to conjure trace energy," she said. "Let me know if you're interested. I cast them around the inn on a regular basis. Guests can usually feel the magical traces and that keeps them on good behavior."

"I am. Interested I mean. In the spells," Drew babbled, backing up to keep from staring down at her exposed cleavage. The last person he needed to be ogling was Noel Townsend. "I'll be in touch."

Before she could say anything else, he hightailed it back out onto the street and sucked in a deep breath of the cool late-autumn air. "Christ, Andrew, get yourself together, man," he mumbled under his breath.

"You all right, Drew?" a woman asked from behind him.

He turned around and spotted Miss Maple. She wore a red and white knit cap over her curly gray hair, green stockings, and was bundled up in a red wool coat. Every year since he could remember, she'd dressed in the same uniform for the entire month of December. When he'd been a kid, he'd been convinced she was one of Santa's helpers. Maybe she was, he mused. Her eyes were twinkling with mischief as she stared at him.

"Woman trouble?" she asked, tucking a few stray locks of hair behind one ear.

"What makes you say that?" he asked, giving her an easy smile.

"In my experience, a man only mutters to himself when he's flummoxed over someone he's attracted to. And since I've never seen you date a man, I'm guessing it's a woman. Is it Shannon?"

"What?" He shook his head. "No, definitely not."

"That's what I thought," she said, her tone unconcerned.

"She's a sweet girl, but subtlety isn't her thing. You might need to be clearer about your intentions."

"I don't have any intentions."

"I know, dear. That's what you need to clear up." She glanced at the inn's front door. Her mouth opened in surprise, and then a knowing look lit her eyes. "Well then. Isn't this interesting?"

"I don't know what you're talking about," he said, shoving his hands into his front pockets. "Listen, Miss Maple, I need to get back to the office. Can I walk you back to your shop?"

She just chuckled and shook her head. "No, dear. I'm fine. Thank you, though."

"You're welcome." He tipped the rim of his ball cap and started to walk across the street.

"Good luck with those woman troubles," Miss Maple called after him.

Without looking back, he raised one hand in acknowledgement and quickened his pace. Miss Maple saw too much. She also presumed more than she should. There wasn't anything going on with Noel Townsend. And there never would be. That wasn't a road he was willing to go down again.

Drew let out a sigh of relief when he stepped back into the sheriff's office. This was his domain. It'd been five years since he'd taken the post in Keating Hollow. Five years of keeping his home town safe.

"Oh, Deputy Baker. There you are," Clarissa, the front desk clerk said. "There's an urgent call for you on line one."

He glanced at the desk phone and the flashing red light. "Who is it?" he asked, already striding toward his office.

"Sheriff Barnes," she said, biting her lower lip. "He just said it was important."

"Thanks." He strode into his office and grabbed the phone. "Baker here."

He stood stock-still as he listened to his boss on the other end of the line. A chill ran through him as he took in the news. Five minutes later, he placed the receiver back down on the phone, straightened his shoulders, and strode back out of his office, heading for the front door.

"Deputy Baker?" Clarissa asked, concern radiating from her. "Is everything okay?"

He paused and glanced at her.

"You look like you've seen a ghost," she said, standing up and pressing her hands flat on her desk. "What happened?"

He shook his head. "I'm fine, Clarissa. I just need to deliver some bad news. I'll fill you in when I get back."

She slowly sat back down and gave him a small nod. She was professional enough to not ask more questions. Not before the family had been notified. It was the part of the job he hated the most. But it *was* his job, and waiting wouldn't make it better.

Steeling himself, he took off and returned to the Keating Hollow Inn. He waited patiently just inside the front door while Noel Townsend checked in an older couple who were celebrating their fiftieth wedding anniversary. The husband kept his hand on the small of his wife's back the entire time, and the pair glowed with so much happiness, Drew couldn't help but smile at them.

"Isn't she lovely," the old man said. "She's still just as gorgeous as she was at sixteen."

"Oh, George." The woman beamed up at him. Then she turned to Drew. "Is it any wonder I married my high school sweetheart?"

Pain struck Drew in the gut as images of Charlotte filled his mind, but he forced a smile and nodded at them. "Happy anniversary, you two."

"Thank you." The woman placed a small hand on his arm and squeezed. Then as she walked by, she whispered, "Don't worry, dear. Your someone is already waiting for you."

Once they disappeared into the elevator, Noel gave him a teasing smile. "She probably means Shannon."

But Drew was all business as he turned to her, his eyes serious as he took his cap off. "Noel, I've got some bad news."

Her smile vanished, and she froze in place. "Is it my dad? Did something happen?"

"No." He shook his head then sucked in a breath. "It's about your husband Xavier. They've found him."

CHAPTER 2

"KEATING HOLLOW INN, how can I help you today?" Noel Townsend said into the phone as she finished typing in the details of a reservation.

"Mommy, guess what!" her sweet six-year-old Daisy yelled, making Noel jerk the receiver away from her ear.

Noel winced even as she grinned, her daughter's joyful exuberance filling her heart. "What is it, baby?" she asked. "Did your aunt finally take you golf cart racing?" Noel's younger sister had moved back to town just a couple months ago and had promptly purchased a party golf cart. Daisy had taken one look and fallen completely in love with its flashing lights and surround sound. And after she'd overheard a conversation about golf cart races, Daisy had become relentless in begging to participate in a race.

"No," Daisy said, her tone turning pouty. "Aunt Abby had to work. She said we can do it this weekend if you say it's okay."

"I see. Well then, what did you call to tell me?"

"Is it okay?" Daisy asked.

"Is what okay?"

"Can I go on the golf cart with Aunt Abby?"

"Right," Noel said with a chuckle. Her daughter definitely had a one-track mind. "Sure, honey."

Daisy let out a shriek of delight. A moment later, Noel heard her older sister, Yvette, say, "Don't forget about the puppy."

"Puppy?" Noel said in alarm, glancing around at her recently remodeled inn. "What puppy?" The gleaming floors had been refinished to perfection. New curtains hung from the floor-to-ceiling windows, pooling at the floor. She'd re-covered her antique furniture, creating the perfect atmosphere for her turn-of-the-century Victorian. It'd taken three years, but her inn was finally exactly how she wanted it. A puppy was the last thing she needed. If Yvette had gifted Daisy with a dog, Noel was going to kill her. Between taking care of Daisy and running the town's only inn, Noel could barely find a spare moment to get her hair cut. Taking care of a puppy was out of the question.

Daisy cooed and said, "Nice puppy. Now be a good girl so Mommy will let you come live with us."

Noel's entire body heated with irritation. She glanced down at the check-in desk, searching for her mobile phone. When she didn't spot the phone right away, she waved her hand, her magic bursting from her fingertips. The air crackled, responding immediately as she said, "Bring me my iPhone."

The stack of papers at the end of the counter lifted into the air, revealing nothing but the wood surface. Her unrefined magic moved on and the papers sailed to the floor. A similar result occurred as her magic searched her desk, scattering pamphlets and advertisements before it moved on to her stack of invoices.

"Damn," she muttered, watching as the front reception area went from organized chaos to something that looked like the

Tasmanian Devil had rolled through. Finally, her magic hovered over her open purse. "Oh, no," she said, her eyes going wide. If the spell upended her bag, her entire life would scatter across the floor. But to her surprise, her magic dipped down and carefully retrieved her phone from her purse. It sailed neatly into her hand.

Noel hit Yvette's phone number as her daughter quipped, "Grandpa got me a puppy. And I loooove her."

"I didn't do it!" Yvette said the second she answered her phone.

"So I hear. Dad did this? Has he lost his mind?" Noel said to Yvette. Then she put the landline receiver back up to her mouth and said, "Is Grandpa keeping the puppy at his house?"

"No. She's mine. He said so," her daughter whined.

Noel tightened her grip on the receiver. "I don't recall anyone asking me, Daisy. We'll have to talk about this when I come to pick you up."

"Mommmm. She needs me."

"I'm sure you think so, sweetheart. But I already said we'll talk about it when I get there."

"But—"

"If you push me, Daisy, the answer is no." Noel stared at the ceiling, hating that she sounded just like her own mother when she herself had begged for a puppy when she was a little girl. She still remembered the temper tantrum she'd thrown when she'd been denied the dog she'd wanted to adopt. But she and Daisy didn't live on a farm near the woods. They lived in an inn and had guests to cater to. Taking in a dog was a huge commitment. "Do you understand?"

"Yes, Mommy," her daughter said. A second later, a clanging sound rang in Noel's ear, followed by Daisy complaining loudly that life was so unfair.

Daisy's dramatics made Noel chuckle as she pressed her

iPhone to her ear and asked Yvette, "What kind of puppy did Dad just bestow on me?"

"I'm not really sure," her older sister said. "Right now, she's just an adorable ball of fluff. Two puppies showed up on his doorstep. Faith's keeping one, and he gave the other one to you."

"How come you didn't end up with one?" Noel asked, narrowing her eyes.

"Isaac's allergic to dogs."

"Abby can fix that," Noel said reasonably, referring to their younger sister who was a gifted earth witch. "Pretty sure one of her potions would fix your husband right up."

There was silence on the other end of the line.

"Yvette, come on," Noel said. "You know I don't have time for a dog. Between chasing after Daisy and dealing with guests—"

"You know, if these puppies had shown up last month, I would've taken one in a heartbeat. But things are... a little stressful at home right now. It's just not a good time."

There was something in Yvette's tone that silenced Noel's argument. Her older sister was the strong, confident one, the one who had the perfect husband and marriage. Everyone loved Isaac. If things were stressful at home, something serious was going on. "Vette? Are you okay?"

Her sister let out a long sigh. "I just don't know yet."

"Want to talk about it?"

"Not over the phone," Yvette said.

"Coffee later?"

"Maybe tomorrow. I'll call you in the morning, okay?"

"Sure. But if you need anything, you know where to find me," Noel said, wishing she could reach out and give her sister a hug.

Yvette let out a small chuckle. "Chasing a puppy around

the inn?"

"Goddess no. That isn't going to work out. We have guests this week. Dad's just gonna have to keep the dog until it's trained."

"Good luck with that. See you tomorrow."

Noel was shaking her head, wondering what the heck she was going to do with a dog, when the bell on the door chimed. An older woman dressed in linen slacks and a silk shirt walked in. Her dyed auburn hair was curled and styled to perfection. An older man who was an inch shorter than her shuffled in behind her. He placed a hand on the small of her back and smiled at Noel as they made their way to the check in counter.

"Mr. and Mrs. Vincent?" Noel asked, expecting them.

"That's us." The woman's clear blue eyes twinkled with happiness.

"Welcome to Keating Hollow." Noel smiled at them and nodded at Alec, her part time helper who was hauling in their luggage. "Take those to the honeymoon suite."

Mrs. Vincent giggled and pressed her hand to her husband's chest. "You booked us the honeymoon suite?"

"Anything for my bride." He tucked a strand of her hair behind her ear. The gesture was so tender, Noel quickly turned to the computer, feeling as if she was intruding on a private moment. She made herself busy processing their check-in, then smiled again as she handed the sweet couple their room key. "You two don't get into any trouble now, you hear?" She winked at them. "The Keating Hollow Inn is a respectable establishment."

"No promises," Mr. Vincent said, grinning at his bride of fifty years. "The missus here says she's expecting a romantic weekend. I can't disappoint, now can I?"

"Definitely not," Noel said, making a mental note to send a chocolate and champagne basket up to their room. The

Vincents had been married for half a century and still looked like newlyweds. Bittersweet emotion swelled her heart as she glanced away. It was the future she'd hoped for when she'd gotten married just before her daughter was born. But that dream died the moment her husband walked out and never looked back. The sharp pain she usually felt in her gut when she thought of Xavier had lessoned to a dull ache, and for that she was grateful. It was well past time she moved on.

She glanced up, watching the couple make their way to the elevator, and spotted Deputy Baker standing near the front door, his arms crossed over his chest. When had he slipped in? Had the bell chimed? She hadn't heard it.

Tall, lean, and broad shouldered, the man was too damned good looking for his own good. And he was also off-limits. He'd made that perfectly clear years ago after a summer when they'd gotten entirely too close. They'd ended up in each other's arms, engaged in an impressive make out session, when he'd pulled back and told her that getting involved would be a big mistake. His rejection had been a blow, but she'd gotten over it. What hurt more was the cooled friendship. These days she wasn't in the market anyway. Once her husband had disappeared, she'd sworn off men. Her attention was reserved solely for her six-year-old daughter, Daisy.

Noel started to ask the deputy what she could do for him, but as the older couple passed him, she heard the woman whisper, "Don't worry, dear. Your someone is already waiting for you."

If Noel hadn't been an air witch, she wouldn't have even heard the comment. But voices carried in the air, giving her heightened hearing, an ability she sometimes resented. She knew she shouldn't stare, should give Drew a hint of privacy, but when his expression turned dark, almost tortured, her heart ached for him. She recognized the look. It was the one he always got when someone mentioned his late girlfriend, Charlotte. There was no doubt in her mind that he was thinking about her. Of course, he was. Charlotte would forever be his *one* who had been taken from him too soon.

"She probably just means Shannon," Noel quipped, trying to lighten the mood. The curvy redhead who worked at A Spoonful of Magic had made her intentions toward the deputy sheriff clear to the whole town, even if it was obvious Drew wasn't interested. Every time Noel spotted him trying to dodge the vivacious vixen, she couldn't help but chuckle. It was his own fault for being gorgeous and too polite to tell her to take a hike.

Drew took his cap off and met her eyes. His haunted expression sent a chill down her spine. "Noel, I'm here on business."

She suddenly found it hard to breathe as fear seized her. She gripped the edge of the counter and automatically asked, "Is it my dad?" Her father was battling cancer, and these days she carried that fear with her at all times. But Drew's news couldn't be about Lincoln Townsend. She'd just been talking with Yvette, who'd been at his house. Surely if something was wrong, she'd have known about it. "What happened?"

"No, it's not your dad," he confirmed and moved closer. "It's about your husband, Xavier. They've found him."

Ex-husband, she immediately thought. Xavier had disappeared on her three years ago. Eighteen months ago, she'd been granted a divorce due to abandonment. Noel blinked, a new kind of fear filtering through her. She must've heard him wrong. "Say that again."

Drew Baker cleared his throat. "I got a call from the county sheriff's office. They found a boat washed up on shore about ten miles north of Trinidad. It was rented by Xavier Anderson seven days ago."

CHAPTER 3

NOEL'S WORLD STOPPED. Her vision narrowed to just Drew, and all she heard was a faint buzzing in her ears. She saw Drew's mouth moving, but she couldn't work out what he was saying. And when she didn't answer him, he strode over behind the desk and placed his hands on her shoulders.

"Come on, Townsend. Snap out of it," he said, leaning down to stare her in the eye. "Don't fall apart on me now."

The sound of his deep voice snapped her back into reality, and she shrugged him off. "I'm fine."

"You sure?" he asked, taking a step back to give her some space.

"I'm sure." She sucked in a deep, cleansing breath. "So, you said they found him. Where is he?"

Drew grimaced. "Eureka. They just identified him this morning."

Raw pain sliced through Noel's heart as she interpreted his words. *Identified.* That meant... "He's dead, then?"

"I'm sorry, Noel," he said, sympathy radiating from his light eyes. "They need you to come confirm his identity."

She gripped the edge of the counter, her fingernails digging into the pine. The pain suddenly turned to a fiery-hot anger. The bastard had been in town last week, and instead of coming to see his daughter, he'd rented a goddamned boat instead. What in the goddess's name was wrong with him? "Where was he?"

"The found him in the boat just above Trinidad."

"I mean," she said, her eyes flashing with rage, "where was he all these years? And what the hell was he doing in Trinidad?"

Drew glanced around the lobby then wrapped his fingers around her elbow and gently guided her toward the front door. "Maybe we should talk about this outside."

"Why?" She dug her heels in and yanked her arm out of his grip. "So the entire town can hear me have a meltdown? What difference does it make, Drew? My daughter is going to grow up knowing her dad not only left her but couldn't be bothered to come see her when he was less than thirty miles away. Do you know what that's going to do to her?"

"I can imagine."

She scoffed, anger taking over and fueling her outburst. "No, you can't. Your parents live here in town. My mom up and left when I was ten. It destroyed me that she never came back, never called, never cared about her girls enough to even send an effing birthday card. And ever since Xavier left, I've prayed he'd come back. Not for me, but for Daisy. She's never gotten over him leaving. Now I don't know that she ever will."

Noel grabbed her phone and sent a quick text to Alec asking him to take care of the champagne basket for the Vincents and letting him know she had to step out for a while. Without waiting for his reply, she grabbed her purse off the desk then stormed out of the inn. The door slammed behind her, but she barely noticed as she stalked across the street and headed for Deputy Baker's patrol vehicle. It was a white SUV with the words *Keating Hollow Sheriff's Department* on the doors.

The chill in the early December air normally would've had her shivering, but she was too numb to notice. Grabbing her coat hadn't even crossed her mind. She heard Drew's heavy footsteps behind her and quickened her pace. She wasn't in any hurry to identify her ex-husband's body, but she had to move. She wanted to throw things, to scream at the top of her lungs. Instead, she fumed silently, her arms crossed over her chest as she waited for Drew to unlock the passenger door.

He didn't say anything as he held the door open for her or when he slid into the driver's side. But he did silently take her hand in his as he put the car in gear and sped out of town.

Noel stared down at their connection, her eyes focusing on his strong, slender fingers. How long had it been since she'd allowed a man to hold her hand? Not since Xavier, she was sure of it. She'd been on a couple of dates in the last year or so, but neither had gotten past the awkward first date. Both had been nice guys, she just hadn't been ready for any kind of relationship. She'd only had room in her heart for Daisy and her family. And while she thought it should feel strange and uncomfortable to let Deputy Baker hold her hand, the reality was neither of those things. Despite his desire to keep a certain amount of distance between them, Drew was still a friend, and had been for the past ten years.

She lightly squeezed his hand and said, "Thank you."

"No need to thank me. Just doing my job." He glanced across the car and gave her a small smile.

Noel shook her head. "I highly doubt holding my hand while you drive me to the morgue is in your job description. If you want to play it cool, then have at it *Deputy Baker*, but we both know I probably should've just driven myself."

"No way, Noel. Not while you're in shock. Besides," he glanced over at her, "you did sort of demand I do it."

"I did not." She tried to pull her hand from his, but he tightened his grip.

"Yes, you did. What do you call stomping over to my car and waiting at the door? Do you really think I'd have ever denied you a ride to Eureka?" He gave her an incredulous look.

"You should have. It's not like I don't have a perfectly good SUV sitting at my inn." She stared at their hands again. "You can let go. While I appreciate the support, I think I can handle things now."

His gaze drifted to their joined hands and for a moment, she thought he was going to refuse. But he frowned and released his hold. "Sorry about that. Overprotective nature, I guess."

"I'd say so," she said, her hand suddenly feeling cold and abandoned. She gritted her teeth and gave herself a tiny shake. *Snap out of it, Noel,* she told herself. He's just a casual friend. Nothing else. But that was a lie, too. They'd been *best* friends at one point in their lives. And she was willing to bet he still knew her better than anyone, even though they'd made a pointed effort to keep their distance.

"Sorry," he said again and steered the car expertly down the winding, two-lane road that headed toward the coast.

They were surrounded by majestic redwoods, and in the distance there were rolling hills, followed by the Pacific Ocean. The image of Xavier lying face down in some charter boat sent a chill through her, and she wrapped her arms around her body.

"Are you cold?" he asked, already reaching for the heater controls. "You should've brought a jacket."

"No." She shook her head, glancing down at herself. She was wearing a green sweater, jeans, and leather boots. He was right. It was December on the Northern California coast. She should've brought a jacket, but the truth was she was in shock. She could barely feel anything. A jacket wasn't going to help her.

"Well, I am," he said and flipped the heat on.

If she hadn't seen him reach over and work the controls, she never would've noticed the warm air. She turned her head and stared out the window. The gorgeous redwoods lining the highway usually captivated her. Not today. All she could think about was Xavier, his sandy blond hair, bright green eyes, and easy smile. She was smitten from the very first time she'd laid eyes on him. He'd been easy going, fun, full of life. He'd brought her out of her shell during a time in her life when she'd felt as if she'd been drowning. Yvette had just gotten married. Abby was living in New Orleans and hadn't been home in three years. Faith had just left for college. And her dad had thrown himself into work at his brewery. The only person still in town who she'd been close to was Drew, and he'd long ago put the brakes on their friendship after a night of drinking that had led to an ill-advised make-out session.

Noel had been contemplating leaving Keating Hollow, but then Xavier had walked into the brewery and everything had changed. Her life had been like a dream for four years. Then it had turned into a nightmare.

She clenched her fists, anger coiling in her gut. "How dare he?" she said out loud to no one.

"How dare he what?" Drew asked.

She whipped her head around, her insides churning with bitterness. "How dare he die without giving me answers."

Drew opened his mouth to say something, probably to soothe her, but she raised her hand, stopping him.

"Don't," she said, her voice low and full of steel. "You don't have the answers any more than I do. There's nothing to say."

"There's always something to say, Noel."

She glanced up at him and shook her head. "Not this time."

His hands tightened around the wheel, and she knew he was dying to contradict her, but when he didn't say anything else, she knew in her soul she was right. There was no defense for a man who'd walked out on his three-year-old daughter and never looked back.

CHAPTER 4

DREW STOOD RIGHT behind Noel in front of the coroner's office. She'd stopped a couple of feet away from the door, her body frozen as if she couldn't take one more step. The air seemed to crackle around her and her blond hair was full of static electricity. It was likely her air magic was charged from her stress. It happened. Too much emotion effected magic in different ways. He just hoped for both their sakes that she kept it under control.

"You can do this, Noel," he said into her ear, hoping a little encouragement would calm her.

"I—I really don't think I can," she said, her voice shaking. "This was the last thing I expected to be doing today."

"I know," he said gently. "No one ever expects to have to do this. But the sooner we go in, the sooner it will be over with. You're strong, Noel. I know you can do this. I'll do it with you. Ready?"

She sucked in a deep breath and then let it out in a long sigh. "No. I'll never be ready."

He reached up and ran his hands down her arms. Her

power buzzed lightly under his palms. She stiffened, clearly not expecting the contact, and then took two decisive steps forward and pulled the glass door open.

"You coming?" She glanced back at him, one eyebrow raised.

"Yep." He hurried after her into the drab office. Everything was beige; the walls, the floors, the uniforms. Even the sound of the receptionist's voice was dull.

"Name?" the woman said without looking up from her computer.

"Noel Townsend is here to identify her ex-husband, Xavier Anderson," Drew said.

She finally looked up, scanned Drew, and asked, "And you are?"

"Deputy Baker from Keating Hollow."

She took her sweet time typing their information into the computer. Drew watched as she pecked around like a chicken using only her two index fingers. Damn, he thought. Was the hiring pool so bad that they couldn't even find a receptionist who could type?

Noel worried the hem of her green sweater as she rocked back on her heels. Then she started to tap her foot and drum her fingers on the counter.

"Could you stop that?" the receptionist asked, annoyance coloring her tone. "I'm trying to concentrate."

"Is that what you call it?" Noel asked, staring straight at her.

The receptionist bristled, glared at Noel, and then deliberately started to type slower. Drew ground his teeth together. If his receptionist behaved that way, she'd find herself on the unemployment line. He couldn't believe this was the first contact when the public had to come identify a loved one. Even though Xavier Anderson was Noel's ex-husband, he was still the father of her child, and she'd loved him once. Finding out he'd died was still traumatic.

"For the love of—" Noel started.

"Oh, Baker, you're here," a man with a gruff voice said from behind them.

Drew turned around and nodded at Coroner Fisk. Unfortunately, it wasn't the first time he'd had reason to visit the man's office. Drew nodded and gestured to Noel. "This is Noel Townsend."

"Ms. Townsend. I'm sorry for the unpleasantness of this situation, but it is an honor to meet you." He held his hand out and shook Noel's. "Ready?"

"As ready as I'm going to be," she said, gripping Drew's arm so tight, he thought he might lose the feeling in his hand. But he didn't care in the slightest. She could've ripped the limb right off, and he wouldn't have said a word. He knew all too well what it was like to lose someone important. Drew stayed glued to her side as they made their way back to the morgue.

"We think he'd been washed up on shore for less than twelve hours. But he's been dead for at least three days. No real trauma was evident, so you won't have to deal with a mangled corpse."

Noel tripped over nothing when he said the words 'mangled corpse' and clutched Drew's arm harder with both hands to keep from going down. Drew quickly reached out with his other hand and helped steady her.

"You're okay," he whispered in her ear, wishing there was something he could do to take on this burden for her.

She nodded and squared her shoulders, a fierce look of pure determination settling on her delicate features. That was the Noel Townsend he knew so well.

"Of course, that does mean we need to run an autopsy to find out what happened," Fisk rattled on. He glanced over his shoulder at her. "Did he have any enemies that you know of? Any reason to expect foul play?"

Noel shrugged. "No idea. I haven't seen him in over three years."

"Oh. I see." Fisk met Drew's gaze. "You did say *ex-wife*, didn't you?

Drew nodded. "His daughter is next of kin, but she's only six. Xavier Anderson doesn't have any other family on record."

"Okay." Fisk opened the door and ushered them into the sterile room.

The air was so cold, and Drew couldn't stop the shiver that crawled over his skin. But Noel didn't seem to notice. She stood in the middle of the room, her eyes trained on the table and body covered with a drop cloth.

"Are you ready for this?" Fisk asked her, moving to stand on the other side of the table.

She choked out a short, "Yes."

It was then Drew realized she was trembling. But considering a sheen of sweat had popped out on her forehead, he didn't think it was from the cold.

Fisk reached for the sheet and lifted it just enough to show Noel the man's face.

Noel let out a little gasp, blinked twice, then shook her head as she glanced away. Her complexion turned so pale, Drew took a step forward, worried she might pass out.

"It's not Xavier," she said.

"It's not?" Fisk asked, his eyebrows disappearing under his thick dark hair. "Are you sure?"

The trembling stopped as she straightened her shoulders and stared him in the eye. There wasn't anything weak about her when she said, "I'm positive. I'd know the father of my child, Mr. Fisk. So unless you have another dead man around here you want me to take a look at, I think we're done here."

Drew couldn't help but admire her fierceness. She always had been a force to be reckoned with.

Fisk led the way back out of the morgue and gestured for them to follow him to a small, windowless office. "Wait here," he said and disappeared inside. A minute later, he reappeared and waved them in. "Deputy Sheriff Reilly is here. He'd like to have a word with you before you go."

Deputy Sheriff Reilly? What the hell was that jackass doing there? Reilly worked directly under county Sheriff Barnes. If Barnes had sent Reilly, did that mean they thought there was foul play? If so, what could it possibly have to do with Noel since she didn't even know the man on the table?

"Have a seat, Ms. Townsend," Reilly said to Noel. The skinny, balding man sat in the leather chair, his elbows propped on the metal desk.

"I'll stand if you don't mind," she said, shoving her hands into her jean pockets.

"Suit yourself." Reilly sat back in the leather chair, kicked his feet up onto the desk, and locked his fingers behind his neck. "Have you ever seen that man before?"

"No."

"Are you positive, Ms. Townsend? If you're not being truthful, this could end badly for you." Reilly studied her with hardened eyes as if she was some sort of suspect.

His demeanor pissed Drew off. He was about to tell the jackass to cool it when Noel said, "Sir, I already told you I don't know him." She turned to Drew and asked, "Do I have to be here?"

Drew shook his head, holding his hand out to her. "No. We can go."

She slipped her hand into his, and he tightened his fingers around her chilled ones. He started to tug her out of the room.

Reilly stood, grabbed something out of his top drawer and

waved it at them. "The John Doe in there was found with Xavier Anderson's wallet. There's even a picture of you and a little girl inside." He flipped it open to the driver's license. "You're telling me the man in this picture isn't the man lying on that table?"

Noel leaned in and studied the ID. Then she jerked back, her eyes wide and full of something Drew couldn't quite place. Fear? Shock? Confusion? "That ID is current," she finally said.

Reilly glanced at it. "So it is. But you still didn't answer my question. Is the man in this picture your husband?"

"Ex-husband," Noel said through clenched teeth. "But yes, that's him."

"And you're saying the man on the table isn't this man?" Reilly peered at the ID.

"Yes. That is exactly what I'm saying." Noel glowered at him. "Frankly, Deputy, I'm surprised you can't tell the difference."

Reilly pursed his lips in concentration, then shrugged. "I guess I see what you mean. But John Doe in there looks kind of like him. Both have blond hair anyway. He could've easily passed as Mr. Anderson."

Drew had the intense urge to clock Reilly. What was he doing? There was no reason to believe Noel knew anything about this situation. Instead, he just tightened his hold on Noel's hand, making sure she knew she wasn't alone.

"What are you trying to tell me, Deputy?" Noel asked. "That Xavier's identity has been stolen?"

"That's a strong possibility." He ran a hand over his angular jaw. "If you hear from your husband or have any idea where he might be, make sure you get in touch with me as soon as possible. He might be the only one who'll be able to shine a light on our John Doe."

Noel's eyes narrowed, and Drew could feel the ire rolling

off her. *"Ex-husband.* I already told you that I haven't seen or heard from him in three years. That isn't a lie, and I have no reason to believe he'll contact me. But if you find him, please do let me know. I wouldn't mind collecting the child support he owes me."

"Oh, we'll find him. Don't you worry about that. But we're going to need a better picture than this." He tapped the wallet. "You'll need to supply us with the most recent pictures you have. One with a full-face view and a profile view if you have them."

"I don't..." She shook her head, clearly frustrated, then said, "Fine. I'll give them to Deputy Baker."

"Good. A word of caution; don't drag your feet on this. The bosses won't be happy, and you won't want to deal with that shit storm. We need them as soon as possible. Tomorrow at the latest."

Her body tensed as she visibly seethed, and Drew couldn't blame her. Why was she being treated like a criminal?

"Let's go," Drew said, glaring at Reilly. Drew knew the man had a job to do, but there was no reason to keep pushing Noel. Not after she'd just stared death in the face. "We're done."

Reilly shrugged one shoulder and sat back down as if he didn't see any issue with his behavior.

Drew let out a huff of disgust as he shuffled Noel out of the building.

Once they were outside, Noel pulled her hand from his and waited without a word as Drew unlocked and opened the passenger door for her. After she was tucked inside, he jogged to the driver's side and jumped in. He cranked the engine, slammed the car into gear, and pealed out of the parking lot.

He weaved in and out of traffic, putting as much distance as he could between them and the coroner's office as quickly as possible. He didn't want to admit it, but there was no denying that the experience had shaken him. Being a deputy sheriff, he wasn't a stranger to death, but watching Noel process the possible loss of a loved one had brought back memories he'd long ago buried. Images of Charlotte lying lifeless in Abby Townsend's work shed flooded his brain and made his pulse quicken. A pit formed in his stomach as bile rose up in the back of his throat. He tightened his grip on the steering wheel and headed north, lost in his own thoughts.

In no time, he was back on highway 299, headed toward Keating Hollow. Everyone who lived in their magical village knew the highway like the back of their hand, and Drew was no exception. He stepped on the gas, taking the curves with expert precision.

Next to him, Noel sucked in a sharp breath.

Without taking his eyes off the road, he asked, "Are you okay?"

"I will be."

It was the tremble in her voice that got his attention. He glanced over. She'd turned a sickly shade of pale green and was holding her stomach. "Whoa." Drew quickly pulled the car off to the side of the road.

Noel burst from the vehicle and stumbled down the side of the bank toward the river. Drew ran after her, cursing himself, and caught up just as she fell to her knees and started to retch.

"I'm so sorry, Noel," he said, kneeling beside her.

She tried to shake her head, but the retching continued.

Drew carefully pulled her hair back and lightly rubbed her back as he patiently waited for her to empty her stomach.

"Oh, goddess," she finally whispered and glanced up at him through watering eyes. "I'm the one who should be sorry. I can't believe I did this."

"Nothing to be sorry about." He stood and offered his hand.

Noel let him pull her to her feet. He gently guided her over to the water's edge, pulled a handkerchief out of his back pocket, and proceeded to dunk it into the river. He held the bundle in his hands and whispered, *"Vapos."*

The icy water heated instantly from his magic, and steam rose from the cloth as he handed it to her. Even though he was a powerful water witch, he didn't have cause to use his power much. He was pleased he'd been able to call up the spell so readily after being out of practice.

"Thank you," she said and took a moment to clean herself up. When she was done, her cheeks were rosy from the warmth of his handkerchief. "I'm okay now."

But she wasn't. Her cheeks might have been warm, but the rest of her was shivering and she was unsteady on her feet. Drew stripped his jacket off and wrapped it around her shoulders.

"I'm fine," she said, trying to shrug the jacket off.

"Noel," he said, his tone gentle. "It's okay to accept help from an old friend."

She stared up at him, raw emotion radiating in her big blue eyes. She opened her mouth to speak, but the words seemed to get caught in her throat.

Drew opened his arms and said, "Come here."

Noel's head dropped, but she walked forward and wrapped her arms around him. He held her, resting his cheek on the top of her head as he murmured soothing words.

Her hands fisted in his shirt, and her grip tightened as if she were holding on for dear life.

"I've got you, Noel," he whispered. "I won't let go. I promise."

She nodded and buried her head into his shoulder.

Drew would've given anything to take her pain away. To save her from more trauma. He'd been there for her, of course, when her husband disappeared three years ago. He'd been the one to take the missing persons report when she'd been angry and scared and unable to believe he'd just walk out without so much as a goodbye. No one had really believed he'd left of his own free will. She and Xavier had seemed like the perfect, all-American couple. From afar, Xavier had seemed like a devoted father and family man. It wasn't unusual to see the three of them around town, to see Xavier taking his daughter to the park or to A Spoonful of Magic.

But when it was discovered Xavier had packed a suitcase and then cleaned out most of their savings a week later, there hadn't been any question that Xavier Anderson had left on his own—no note, no phone call, no nothing. And suddenly Noel had found herself a single mother with no answers. She'd changed after that. Her infectious smiles had become rare unless she was playing with her daughter, and she no longer radiated with the openness that had drawn him to her ten years ago. Her heart had been broken, and it was clear to everyone who loved her—including him—that it had never healed.

"I'm so sorry, Drew," she finally said, pulling out of his embrace. "I don't know what happened. I never get car sick."

He gave her a sympathetic smile. "Maybe if I hadn't been driving like a bat out of hell, you wouldn't have lost your lunch."

"That wasn't it and you know it," she said, stuffing her hands in her pockets. "It was the—"

He held up a hand stopping her. "I know. Getting queasy is pretty normal after a trip to the morgue. There's no need to explain."

She was silent for a moment then gave him a small nod. "Thanks. I'm ready to get back on the road. I need to get home so I can clean myself up before I go get Daisy from my dad's house."

"Sure." He grabbed her hand again and helped steady her as she climbed back up the bank.

The passenger door to his SUV was still wide open, and she grimaced. "Sorry," she said again when he was back in the driver's seat.

"If you apologize one more time, you're going to piss me off," he said with a mock scowl as he turned the engine over and then blasted the heat.

"Right," she said, buckling her seatbelt. "No more apologies."

"Thank you." He eased the vehicle back out onto the road, this time careful to keep the speed within the legal limit.

They were both quiet as the daylight rapidly disappeared and turned to dusk. By the time they made it back to Keating Hollow night had fallen, and Main Street was lit up with festive holiday lights. Just as they passed the inn, Noel said, "You can let me out here."

Drew shook his head as he pulled into the small parking lot around the back and killed the engine. "You still have to get Daisy, right?"

"Um, yeah," she said hesitantly. "But I'm good. I can drive myself."

"I'd rather you didn't. I'd feel more comfortable if you just let me drive you to your dad's house."

"Drew," she said. "Please don't make a big deal out of what happened back there. I'm perfectly fine now. I just... well, I was in shock, I guess. Though I shouldn't be, right? I mean, nothing's changed when it comes to Xavier. He still left us, only now it appears he's had his identity stolen. Not my concern or my business." Her eyes narrowed, and her voice took on a hard edge. "Though the fact that he's obviously been near Keating Hollow and hasn't come to see his daughter—"

She abruptly closed her mouth, shook her head, and then

added, "I'm rambling."

He gave her a small smile. "Sounds like you're just getting a few things off your chest."

With a sigh, she nodded. "I guess so."

"Come on. Let's get you inside then I'll take you to get Daisy."

"Drew, my family will be there. I don't want to answer any questions right now. Not yet. I need to process. If you're there, they're going to pepper me with a million and one questions."

"I'll wait in the car. You can tell them you have a dead battery or something and I took pity on you." He climbed out then opened the door for her, determined to not take no for an answer. Because ever since she'd let him hold her, let him soothe her, something had shifted inside of him. An intense need to keep her safe had seized him. And leaving her to drive across town to her family home after she'd been so shaken was out of the question.

"Dead battery?" She glanced at her aging Honda and nodded. "That will work."

The ache in Drew's chest eased as he followed her into the inn.

She led him through the door behind the front desk and into the ground-floor residence she shared with her daughter. The two-bedroom suite was warm and cozy with dark hardwood floors, overstuffed furniture, and pictures everywhere. There were fresh cut lilies on the coffee table along with a pile of books and pillar candles. Noel strode to one of the bedrooms and said, "I'll be right out."

"Take your time. I'm fine here," he said, meaning it. But then he sat down and leaned back into her couch, and her faint citrus scent rose up around him. Long-buried emotions came rushing to the surface. And suddenly all he wanted was to feel her in his arms again.

CHAPTER 5

Normally the twinkle lights that lit up the tree-lined drive of her family home gave Noel a sense of peace. But not tonight. Tonight, she just felt anxious. She didn't know what to make of the revelation that Xavier had likely been in the area. Or the fact that he hadn't gotten in touch with her.

Now she couldn't get the image of him lying dead in an alleyway out of her head. The John Doe had gotten Xavier's wallet somehow. Half of her wanted to jump in her car and start a man hunt until she found him. But the other half, the part that wanted nothing more than to protect her daughter, wanted to block the day from her mind and forget it ever happened.

Besides, if Reilly was serious, the county sheriff's department would be conducting a full-on manhunt for him anyway. She'd already done her part by digging up some photos of him back at the inn. Drew had them now and would hand them over to the investigators.

"Looks like Wanda's here," Drew said, bringing his SUV to a stop.

"Huh?" Noel jerked her head up, scanning the small parking area in front of her dad's lavish log cabin.

"The party golf cart. Seems a little cold for golf cart races."

Noel turned her attention to the six-person party cart her sister had purchased a few weeks ago and snorted. "Oh, no. That's Abby's. She got a cart of her own after Wanda benched her."

"What do you mean 'benched her?'" Drew asked, his forehead wrinkling in confusion.

Noel had a sudden urge to smooth his wrinkles and started to reach up before she stopped herself and clenched her fist. What was she doing? She didn't have a right to touch him. Not like that. They weren't dating, for goddess's sake. He was just being kind to her. "Abby was driving and almost tipped it into the river. Naturally, Wanda took her privileges away. The next day, Abby showed up with this." Noel felt a smile tug at her lips. "I have to admit, it's pretty fun tooling around in that thing."

"Right," Drew said, his expression sour as he glared at the poor golf cart.

"Something wrong? Is there a law on the books about golf cart racing we aren't aware of, Deputy Baker?"

"No." Drew shook his head, still eyeing the cart. His eyes flashed with anger, but when he blinked, all emotion vanished as if he'd just closed the window she'd been peeking in.

"Then what's the problem, Drew?"

"Nothing. I just hope she and Wanda don't cause any trouble on those things."

Noel gave him a puzzled look. What was wrong with him? Half the people in town had their own golf cart. There was even a special road along the river specifically for the things. "Okay. Well, I'm going to get Daisy. I'll be right back."

She left Drew in his vehicle and hurried into her father's house. She recognized the sound of her daughter's laughter coming from the living room, and the heavy weight of the afternoon suddenly vanished. Daisy was the joy in her life, and no matter what was troubling her, when she was with her daughter everything was just better.

"Come here, girl!" Daisy called and clapped her hands. "You can do it. Good puppy."

Noel let out a groan. She'd forgotten all about the puppy phone call earlier in the day. Steeling herself for the fight to come, Noel strolled into the living room.

Daisy was lying on her stomach, her chin propped up on a pillow as she grinned at the little ball of fluff dancing in front of her. The brindle-coated puppy inched closer then darted her tongue out and licked Daisy on the nose. Daisy's eyes twinkled as she giggled, a sound Noel rarely heard these days. Her heart melted into a gooey puddle of love.

Abby glanced up from her spot on the couch and met Noel's gaze. A grin spread across her sister's face as she mouthed, *You're doomed.*

Noel stifled a sigh and nodded her defeat. Of course, she was. How could she deny her daughter the obvious joy of the most adorable puppy that ever lived? "Does this puppy have food? Toys? A crate? Anything to take home with us, or do I need to beg Randy at the pet store to stay open a few minutes longer tonight?"

"Mommy!" Daisy scooped up the puppy with both hands and ran over to her mother, holding the creature out in front of her like an offering. "Isn't she beautiful?"

"She's gorgeous, sweetheart. Have you named her yet?"

Tears filled Daisy's big brown eyes. "I get to keep her?"

"That depends," Noel said, rocking back on her heels.

Daisy clutched the puppy to her chest, cradling her protectively. "What do you mean?"

Noel kneeled down in front of her daughter. Giving Daisy a gentle smile, she swept a lock of her fine dark hair out of her eyes and said, "You have to promise to take care of her. Feed her every day, take her for walks, and clean up after her."

"I will," Daisy said, clutching the puppy tighter, a fat tear rolling down her cheek.

Noel's chest ached as she gently wiped the tear away. "And you have to promise to love her with all your heart."

"I already do." Daisy spun around and ran over to Abby. "Did you hear Mommy? She said I could keep Buffy."

Abby laughed. "I heard her, sweetie pie. Now go tell grandpa the good news and gather her supplies. It's a school night, isn't it?"

Daisy's expression clouded over. "Yeah. School." She glanced down at Buffy. "Think Miss Quinn will let me bring her?"

"She'll have to stay at the inn with me, Daisy," Noel said and tapped her wrist watch. "Get her stuff, we have to get going."

Daisy nodded, still clutching the puppy as she ran toward the kitchen.

"Be careful!" Noel called after her. Daisy slowed to a fast walk then disappeared out the back door.

Noel flopped down on the couch beside her younger sister Abby and pressed her hand to her heart. "Talk about an ambush."

"Yeah, but she's so happy," Abby said, patting her sister's knee. Then she studied her for a moment. "Hey, you dyed your hair blond and added extensions. It looks amazing. What happened to the red?"

"I was tired of getting it touched up every four or five weeks. And I really needed the change." Noel said, shrugging.

She'd been restless lately, and one night she'd looked in the mirror and decided she hated her asymmetrical haircut and the color. So, she did what she always did; she went back to her natural look, the one that made her feel the most like her previous self. The person she'd been before everyone in her life had left her.

"I like it," Abby said with a nod of approval.

"Thanks. I thought I'd try my natural look for a while." Noel leaned back into the cushions and eyed her sister with suspicion. "How did you manage to avoid becoming a new puppy momma?"

"Whoa there," Abby said. "Aren't you forgetting about Endora, Olive's very rambunctious golden retriever?" She raised a hand so it was level with her forehead. "I'm up to here in dog hair and chewed power cables. One more might mean the end of me."

Noel groaned. "Right. I forgot." Then she glanced at her sister's radiant smile and relaxed posture. There was obvious joy written all over her, and suddenly Noel felt sad and empty. She'd been happy like that once. She'd thought she had a lifetime of love ahead of her, a future with a house full of kids and so much love they'd nearly burst from it. Now she was a single mother with a daughter who rarely went a night without waking from a nightmare.

"Hey, where'd you just go?" Abby asked her, concern coloring her tone.

"Nowhere. It's just been a long day is all."

"I have a new energy potion that—"

"I'm okay," Noel said, standing up as Lin Townsend walked in through the backdoor with a brown bag in one hand and a dog crate in the other. Daisy followed behind him, chattering on about how she and Buffy were going to be best friends.

"Of course, you are, sweetheart," Lin said to his granddaughter. Then he gave Noel a sheepish smile.

"I had Clair run out and get you all the supplies you'll need," he said, referring to his longtime girlfriend. He held the bag up, the same twinkle she'd just seen in her daughter's eyes winking back at her. "Puppy food, treats, chew toys, dog brush. There's even a blanket in the crate."

Noel narrowed her eyes and glared at her father. "You didn't think you should ask me first before promising a certain someone a puppy?"

He glanced at Daisy, his expression tender as he said. "Grandpa's privilege."

Abby let out a huff and shook her head. "Dad, you're the worst. What would you have done if Grandma had dumped a puppy off on you when we were kids?"

"What makes you think she didn't?" he asked with one eyebrow raised. "Do you really think I would've willingly chosen Barky for the family pet?"

The image of the mangy mutt who'd been so hyper and out of control that he'd destroyed three fences in six months flashed in Noel's mind. The dog had come to them with tufts of hair missing, a lame paw, and zero manners. They'd managed to fix up his paw and skin issues, but his manners? Not so much. The dog had misbehaved every day of his life, including his last one when he'd dug up most of the winter garden crop just hours before he went to sleep and never woke up.

In the end, old age had taken him—but he'd sure led a full life. That dog had gotten into so much trouble and barely escaped intact so many times, he'd been like a cat with nine lives.

"Grandma's to blame for Barky?" Noel asked incredulously. "Was she insane?"

"I'm saying yes," Lin said, smiling down at his daughter. "That dog showed up on her front porch, and when no one would take him but a kill shelter over in Eureka, she freaked out, drove him over here, and gave him to Yvette. Her face lit up like a Christmas tree, and that was the end of that. No more peace in the Townsend household."

"If *Buffy* is anything like Barky, you're going to owe me restitution."

"Don't worry, Noel," Lin said. "No puppy will ever be as bad as Barky. He took that prize and buried it deep in the orchard."

Lin shuffled over to the kitchen, and Noel couldn't help but notice his movements were slower than they'd been just a few months ago. He appeared to be thinner, more fragile, too. *It's the chemo,* she told herself.

Lin had been diagnosed with cancer three months ago. Leukemia. And the fact that the Townsends were a family of witches didn't mean a damned thing. Abby could make him energy potions, but that was about it. All Noel could do for him was manipulate the air temperature. She was nothing more than a cheaper version of an HVAC system. On any other day, she'd be amused by her self-reflection, but after the day she'd had, everything was just too much.

Emotion crawled up her throat and threatened to choke her. She didn't want to see her father weakened or think about the possibility that Xavier was nearby and actively avoiding her... or worse, dead in a ditch. As much as she resented him for not only leaving, but leaving her the way he did, she still didn't want to see him hurt. And not just for Daisy's sake, but for hers as well. She *had* loved the man.

"Noel?" Abby said, touching her arm. "Something's wrong. What is it?"

"I'm fine," she said, her tone a little too clipped. Abby's concerned expression morphed into a pained one, and Noel cursed herself. Her relationship with Abby was already a little strained. When Abby had packed up and left just after high school graduation, Noel had taken it the hardest. Abby had been her best friend, and when she left, she hadn't just left town. She'd left the entire family, rarely staying in touch or coming home to visit. Noel had often felt as if she'd lost a limb, and the fact that Abby hadn't seemed to feel the same had been like rubbing salt in the wound. Since Abby had moved home two months ago, Noel had been working on letting the past go, but she wasn't always successful.

Tonight was one of those times. The day had overwhelmed her, and all she wanted to do was take her daughter home. "Daisy, let's go, baby."

"Come on, Buffy," Daisy said to the puppy, still clutching her to her chest. Her daughter led the way to the front door while Lin handed Noel the bag of puppy supplies and the crate.

"You'll thank me later." Lin gave his daughter a hug, his embrace stronger than she'd expected. Tears burned her eyes, but she blinked them back. Noel didn't cry. Not in front of other people anyway, and especially not in front of her father. She didn't want him worrying about her while he had so much of his own stuff to deal with.

"I doubt it," she said as she hugged him back, holding on for a few extra moments.

He pulled back and stared down at her. "What's wrong, Noel?"

"Nothing." She shook her head. "Just a long day. Now, I've gotta get Daisy and the *puppy* home."

He studied her for a few seconds more.

Noel kissed him on the cheek and gave him a smile. She let him go and as she walked away, she called over her shoulder, "Night, Dad. Thanks for entertaining Daisy today."

"Any time. You know I love having her over," he said.

Warmth blossomed in Noel's chest at his words, and she waved one last time before she slipped out the front door. Daisy was standing on the porch waiting when Noel finally made it outside. She juggled the bag and puppy crate in one hand and grabbed her daughter's hand with the other. "This way, baby."

CHAPTER 6

DREW GLANCED BACK at Daisy and smiled when he saw the puppy. He'd figured Noel would cave. "Who do we have here?" he asked Daisy.

The little girl let out a yawn as she petted the dog's head. "This is Buffy."

"Buffy?" He laughed. "Who came up with that name?"

"Aunt Abby. She said Buffy was Mommy's favorite."

Drew glanced at Noel with an amused expression. "Buffy... the Vampire Slayer?"

"That's right," someone said just as Noel was about to close her door. Drew peered through the darkness and spotted Abby, the moonlight turning her long blond hair almost silver.

"Holy hell," Noel muttered, clutching her chest with one hand. Clearly Abby had startled her.

Abby leaned down and rested one arm on the open door. "She used to watch that show over and over and over again. I thought the name Buffy might help her take to the puppy sooner."

Drew squinted at Abby in the darkness and felt his insides

go cold. It had been over ten years, and he still found it difficult to be around her. It wasn't something he was proud of; he just couldn't seem to get past the old trauma. Every time he saw her, all he could see was Charlotte's lifeless body in that shed on the Townsend property.

"Hey, Drew. What're you doing out here?" she asked, either unaware of his unease or determined to push through it. He wasn't quite sure which.

Drew cleared his throat. "Noel's battery died. I'm just helping out a friend."

She tilted her head to the side and glanced between him and Noel. "Right, friends."

"Abby," Noel said with a warning in her tone. "Did you need something? I'm exhausted, and it's past Daisy's bedtime."

Abby raised her hands and backed up a step. "Sorry. I didn't mean to hold you up. I just came out to check on you and make sure you're okay. You seem... a little off."

Noel stiffened at her sister's words, and Drew's fingers twitched to take hers in his, to offer his silent support. Instead, he tightened his grip on the steering wheel, keeping his hands to himself.

"I've been 'off' for over a decade, Abby. Or haven't you noticed?" Noel snapped at her sister.

Whoa, Drew thought. What was going on there? Was it possible Noel was still upset that Abby had left town all those years ago? He'd thought they'd made up, but maybe not.

Abby sucked in a sharp breath, her expression shifting from concern to a mixture of hurt and irritation. "Never mind. Forget I asked." She nodded to Drew. "Have a good night, Deputy Baker."

"Goodnight, Abby," Drew called after her.

"Damn," Noel said softly as she watched her younger sister stomp back into the house.

Drew put the SUV into gear and eased down the driveway. He glanced in the rearview mirror and a wave of tenderness washed over him at the sight of Daisy and her puppy, both fast asleep.

"Want to talk about it?" Drew asked her.

"No." Noel crossed her arms over her chest and stared out the window.

"Yeah, I get that. But it's not really healthy to hold on to all that anger. You're probably going to have to forgive her eventually."

Noel snorted. "Have you?"

"Yes," he said simply.

"That's a bunch of bull and you know it," she shot back. "You can't even look her in the eye."

"There might be some truth to that." He turned right at the end of the lane and headed back toward town. "But that doesn't mean I haven't forgiven her. You and I both know what happened with Charlotte wasn't Abby's fault. She doesn't deserve to pay for what happened back then forever, Noel. Hasn't she been through enough? Haven't we all?"

"Yeah," she said into the darkness, but she didn't add anything further.

Charlotte had been Drew's high school sweetheart and Abby's best friend. In the spring of their senior year, Charlotte had come down with some sort of infection and was going to have to miss the prom while she recovered. She'd begged Abby to make her an energy potion so that she wouldn't have to miss out on the celebration. After some persuading from Charlotte, Abby had reluctantly given in to the request.

Drew had taken Charlotte to the prom. It had been a great night... right up until she'd asked him to make a stop at Abby's house. She'd said she just needed to run in and get something. Twenty minutes later when he'd gone to look for her, Drew had found her lifeless in Abby's work shed after snagging and drinking a second batch of the energy potion.

Charlotte hadn't told any of them that she'd had a terminal illness, one she was never going to recover from, and the potion had just been too much for her weakened body. She'd died on the eve of her eighteenth birthday. It was a night that still haunted him.

He supposed it always would.

IT WAS past nine o'clock when Drew walked into the sheriff's office. He sat down at his desk and ran a hand over his head. He'd dropped Noel and Daisy and the new puppy at the inn, promised to check on them the next day, and then headed straight to the office. Sleeping was out of the question. While he'd been waiting outside for Noel at the Townsend residence, he'd had the nagging thought that he had to do something to help her. He knew that Noel was struggling with the fact that Xavier hadn't made contact with them... or more specifically Daisy. And worse, now she had no idea if he was even still alive.

While he'd been sitting in the darkness, Drew had decided he'd do everything in his power to find her ex. One way or another, Drew was going to help Noel get the answers she deserved. And he knew better than most that the county sheriff's office wouldn't make this a priority, no matter what Reilly said. They just didn't have the manpower to devote that much time to a case that had very little evidence.

Drew made a pot of coffee, fired up the computer, and got to work. A half hour later, Drew had sent scans of Xavier's pictures to the county precinct and printed copies of Xavier's new driver's license. He shoved the paperwork and pictures into a file, locked up the office, and headed straight for Keating Hollow Brewery.

The place was owned by Lincoln Townsend but was currently run by Drew's buddy, Clay Garrison. Clay was an earth witch who used his talents to make the best beer on the west coast.

Drew pulled the door open to the brewery and stopped dead in his tracks at the sight in front of him. His buddy had Abby Townsend pressed up against the bar in a steamy lip lock that wasn't safe for G-rated audiences.

Drew cleared his throat loudly.

The couple froze. Then Clay glanced back and said, "Go away."

Abby chuckled softly and slipped out of his embrace. "Drew," she said, eyeing him with suspicion. "Is everything all right with my sister?"

Drew hesitated. Noel hadn't wanted her family to know what she'd been through that day, preferring not to have to answer any questions they had. On the other hand, the news would get out that a dead man had been found in Trinidad. And it was highly likely that because there would be an investigation, Xavier's name would be mentioned. They'd find out eventually. Still, he didn't want to betray Noel's trust.

"Drew?" Abby said again. "What's going on?"

"You should talk to her." Drew strode up to the bar and took a seat.

She was silent as she regarded him, and then she nodded. "I will."

Drew studied her. He'd expected pushback, a demand to be filled in on the details. The Abby he'd known in high school had been relentless. She'd never have given in that easily if she wanted to know something. But as he stared back at her, he saw a maturity and quiet acceptance he hadn't noticed since she'd been back in town. Ten years was a long time. He shouldn't have been surprised by her transformation. God knew he certainly wasn't the same person he'd been back then either.

Abby turned, gave Clay one last kiss, and said, "I'm gonna take off... maybe soak in the tub for a while before you get home."

Clay swept his gaze over her, no doubt imagining her lounging in the bath. Then he pulled her in close and whispered something in her ear.

She gave him a wicked smile and promised to keep the bed warm for him.

Drew averted his gaze and asked, "Are the taps still flowing?"

"Help yourself," Clay said, walking Abby to the door.

How many times had Drew seen them like that in high school? Hundreds. He'd been right beside them, his own arms around Charlotte. The dull ache pulsed in his chest as he filled a twenty-ounce glass with the seasonal porter. He took a seat at the bar and downed nearly half the beer, determined to numb the ache.

The front door clanged shut, and Clay returned to the bar. He glanced at Drew, eyeing his half-empty glass, and started to pour his own porter. "Rough day?"

"Something like that." Drew grimaced and took another gulp of beer.

Clay and Drew had been friends since elementary school. They'd been in more than their share of trouble together. They'd also seen each other through the best and the worst their lives had to offer, so he wasn't surprised when Clay took a seat next to him and said, "Something's definitely got you twisted up. I'd bet a hundred dollars it's Noel."

Drew ground his teeth, irritation making him clench his

fists. "I'd say that's a pretty safe bet since I'm certain Abby told you she saw us together."

Clay chuckled. "Sure, that helps, but that's not why I'd make the bet. The only time I ever see you looking so tortured is after you've run into her. Just own it, man. We both know you want her."

"That's not..." Drew shook his head. "Noel and I don't have that kind of relationship."

He snorted. "No kidding. And that's the entire problem."

Drew downed the rest of his beer, threw a ten on the bar, and stood. He wasn't in the mood for a heart to heart. Not tonight. "Thanks for the beer. I'll see you tomorrow."

"Wait." Clay grabbed Drew's glass and refilled it. Then he shoved the ten back at his friend. "These are on me."

Drew eyed the beer and relented. He couldn't let a good brew go to waste now, could he? "Fine. But stop busting my balls."

Clay's mouth curved into a ghost of a smile. "Sure, buddy. Whatever you say." He lifted his beer in a toast. "To the beautiful Townsend sisters."

"You're a jackass, you know that, right?" Drew said, lifting his glass.

"Well aware." Clay grinned.

Shaking his head, Drew tapped his glass to Clay's and said, "To the beautiful Townsend sisters."

CHAPTER 7

NOEL STOOD in her daughter's bedroom doorway holding a calming potion. Daisy was fast asleep, with Buffy sitting at the edge of the bed, making the most pathetic whining sound.

"Need to go out?" Noel whispered to the puppy.

The dog whined again. Noel set the potion on Daisy's dresser, scooped the puppy up, and headed to the small garden area just off their kitchen. Once she was outside, Noel placed Buffy on the grass and said, "This is where you do your business."

Buffy promptly sat down at Noel's feet and stared up at her with big puppy dog eyes.

Noel sighed. "Really?"

The dog thumped her tail and jumped up on Noel's ankle.

"Come on." Noel led the puppy around the small lawn area for what seemed like forever until the dog squatted. "Good girl. First try and everything." Noel cooed and scooped her back up. "Just like that every time, okay?"

Once they were back inside, Noel rewarded the puppy with one of the dog treats her father had supplied, and then took her back to Daisy's room. She placed the puppy in the crate at the foot of Daisy's bed and whispered, "Now go to sleep. I'll see you both in the morning."

As soon as Noel closed the door to the crate, Buffy started to whine. Noel took one look at her peacefully sleeping daughter and released the puppy. "This is not going to work," she said to the dog. "Come on, you."

Noel crept out of the room with the puppy in one hand and the crate in the other.

Exhaustion took over and her eyes watered as she yawned. All she wanted to do was collapse into bed, but first she needed to shower the morgue memories away. The image of the dead man flashed in her mind. Every detail was crystal clear; his round lifeless eyes, blue lips, and puffy cheeks. He didn't look anything like Xavier, but she had a feeling she'd remember his face for the rest of her life.

She carted Buffy into her bathroom and set her on the floor. Then she quickly undressed and climbed into the shower, where she just stood, letting the scalding water cleanse her soul. When she finally emerged, she wrapped herself in a thick cotton robe and shuffled into her small kitchen with Buffy trailing behind her, and she made herself a cup of hot chocolate.

She was standing at her counter, stirring her cocoa, when she heard a small *yelp* from Buffy. She glanced around the kitchen, finding the puppy wedged between the wall and an indoor ficus tree. She chuckled, freed Buffy, and retreated to the couch in the living room. She glanced down at the dog. "Looks like you're gonna need a wee bit more supervision."

Buffy responded by curling into a ball on Noel's lap and promptly going to sleep.

"Figures." Noel petted the dog, then leaned back into the couch pillows.

As she sipped her cocoa, her gaze landed on the coffee table and the open box full of pictures. She'd left them there after hastily choosing a couple for Drew to give to the county sheriff's office. It was a box she hadn't opened in three years. Now that she had, she couldn't stop herself from taking a trip down memory lane.

It was a mistake.

Seeing their former life, the hope and happiness, Xavier smiling at Daisy with obvious love in his eyes, sent a lightning bolt of pain through her that knocked the wind out of her. She hunched forward, barely getting the mug of cocoa onto the table before it toppled to the floor. Her insides ached, and she gasped for air.

Dammit! What had she been thinking? This was exactly why she'd closed the door on her past. Xavier had taken enough from her already; she wasn't willing to let his memory take even more. She slammed the lid on the box, startling Buffy. The dog lifted her head as Noel shoved the box under the couch. Out of sight, out of mind.

If only it were that easy.

She soothed the puppy. When Buffy settled, Noel leaned into the pillows and closed her tired eyes.

Noel woke with a start, her heart racing at the sound of her daughter's cries.

The sobbing was louder than usual, more frantic, almost panicked. Noel leaped off the couch and ran into Daisy's room. Her daughter was sitting up in bed, gasping for air as she frantically searched the end of the bed.

"She's gone! I can't find her." Daisy turned her tear-stained gaze on Noel. "Mommy, where is she?"

Noel clutched at her chest, realizing the problem. Daisy was near hysterics because Buffy wasn't there. "She's in the living room, love. I'll go get her."

But Daisy didn't wait. She flew out of her bed and ran into the other room. "Buffy!" She hiccupped through her tears and forced out. "Don't—don't leave me like that."

Noel followed her daughter, but just as she was about to leave the bedroom, she spotted the full bottle of calming potion. Damn, she'd forgotten to give it to Daisy. No wonder she'd woken in a panic.

Fat tears rolled down Daisy's cheeks as she clutched the puppy to her chest as if holding on for dear life.

Noel's heart nearly cracked wide open. She grabbed the potion and joined her daughter on the couch. She placed the bottle on the end table and then wrapped her arms around Daisy. The little girl cried softly while snuggling the puppy. Noel rocked her gently and muttered quiet reassurances that she was going to be okay, just as she did every time her daughter suffered a nighttime anxiety attack. They'd started shortly after Xavier left them. Daisy would go to sleep, and almost every night she'd wake up panicked, looking for her mother. Daisy's therapist kept saying Daisy would grow out of them, but Noel was skeptical. Unless someone spelled Daisy to suppress her dreams, Noel highly doubted it. The new calming potion Abby had made for her was helping, but it wasn't a sure thing, and definitely not when Noel forgot to give it to Daisy.

Her daughter's cries finally quieted, and Noel pulled back just enough to glance down at her. Daisy's eyes were closed, and her breathing had evened out. "Asleep already, love?" she whispered and gently brushed her dark curls to the side.

Daisy didn't even move.

Noel glanced at the puppy curled on Daisy's lap and sighed. It looked like she was going to have two extra bed partners. She set Buffy on the floor, grabbed the potion, then stood up, still holding Daisy. She carried her child to her bedroom and said, "Come on, Buffy. Time to go back to bed."

The dog obeyed, trotting along beside her as if she already knew where they were headed. "Smart, aren't you?" Noel said as she placed Daisy into the bed.

Her daughter stirred and blinked up at her. "Where's Buffy?"

"Here you go, love." Noel handed her the dog and then held out the potion. "Drink this before you go back to sleep."

Daisy did as she was told without question and then snuggled down into the covers. The dog jumped to her feet, turned around three times, and then laid back down, placing her head on the pillow right beside Daisy.

Noel couldn't help but smile down at them. She didn't think she'd ever seen anything sweeter in her entire life. With her heart a little less bruised, she climbed in beside them, gave them both kisses, then closed her eyes and let the night take her.

CHAPTER 8

"Noel? Where are you?"

Footsteps sounded on the wood floors, waking Noel from a deep and dreamless sleep. She sat straight up, squinting as the sun streaming through the window blinded her.

"Abby?" Noel called back, rubbing her eyes. "I'm up. What's going on?"

"Noel?" Abby poked her head into her sister's room. Her blond hair was pulled up into a messy bun and she was wearing her work apron as if she'd hurried over from her studio. "Are you feeling okay?"

"Yes. I think so," she said through a yawn. "Why?"

"It's almost ten. Some of your guests are down at the café complaining about the lack of breakfast."

Noel bolted upright and glanced at the clock. It read 9:47. "Holy hell!" She shot out of bed and ran into the bathroom. Less than two minutes later, she ran back out and pulled on a pair of jeans and the nearest sweatshirt. "Daisy, do you have your shoes on?"

"I already took Daisy to school," Abby called from the living room.

Noel froze, her body still pumping with adrenaline. Then she moved to stand in the threshold of her bedroom door and stared at her sister who was sitting in the middle of her hardwood floor petting Buffy. Even though she was wearing old faded jeans and a Keating Hollow Brewery T-shirt under her apron, she looked as gorgeous as ever. Her brilliant blue eyes were striking, and her cheeks were naturally tinted pink, giving her that girl-next-door look. "What do you mean you already took her to school?"

She shrugged. "You were out. Like totally out. When I tried to wake you, you waved me off and rolled over. So I packed her a lunch, made sure she had breakfast, and took her to school. I left you a note, but clearly you didn't see it." She climbed to her feet and pointed to a piece of paper on the coffee table. "What's going on? Are you sick?"

Noel moved to the couch and slowly sank into the cushions while pressing her hands to her forehead. "No. I just—damn." She glanced up at Abby. "I can't believe you strolled right in here, gathered up my daughter, and left without me ever knowing a thing. Me! I'm an air witch. I *hear* everything."

Abby just shrugged. "You should probably get a healer to check that out."

Noel curled her hands into fists and fought the urge to scream. What was going on? She never overslept, and her magic had never failed her before. She simply couldn't understand how she hadn't heard her sister or Daisy that morning. She stood and took a deep breath. "Thank you for getting Daisy off to school. I owe you one."

"No, you don't," Abby said with a laugh. "That's what sisters do, you know. We help each other out. Now, how about we get some breakfast and you can tell me all about Deputy Baker and why you were rolling around in his cruiser last night." She flashed Noel a mischievous smile. "Did you see what's under his hood? Is that why you slept the morning away?"

Noel scowled. "You don't know what you're talking about."

Abby's grin vanished as she stared intently at her sister. "You're right. I clearly don't. Why don't you let me get you some breakfast while you tell me what's going on?"

"There's nothing—"

"Noel," Abby said with an exasperated sigh. "I saw Drew last night at the brewery. He wouldn't say what's going on, but I know something's up. You don't have to tell me, but I wish you would."

The concern on Abby's face penetrated Noel's defenses. Her protective shields vanished and suddenly she was transported back to a time when she and Abby told each other everything. She wanted to talk to her, to feel that closeness again. She just wasn't sure she could. Trust was hard to come by these days. Still, she didn't want to be closed-off. She had to try. Nodding, she said, "Coffee first."

"Thank fate," Abby said, a small smile curving her lips. "I brought coffee over this morning, but when you weren't awake and I found Daisy still in her pajamas playing with the puppy, it was full speed ahead to get her off to school. I forgot all about it. If I don't get caffeine soon, bad things will happen."

Noel scoffed. "Please. You're as perky as ever."

"Perky?" Abby tossed Noel her jacket. "Since when have I ever been *perky*? You were the cheerleader."

"Only because I wanted to show off for Trent Stevens," she shot back, laughing, but then she winced at the memory. Noel had been all arms and legs in high school and had no business trying to dance in public. "They made me cheer in the back of the formation so no one would see how bad I was."

Abby snorted. "You weren't completely awful."

"Really?" Noel pushed her sleeve up, revealing a faded scar on her forearm. "I got this because I couldn't remember right from left and ran smack into Shannon's high kick. I landed on my side and ended up with a broken wrist."

"Oh, that's right." Abby nudged her with her elbow. "Someone should've taken your pompoms away."

Noel scooped up Buffy, took her out, then brought her back in and secured her in the kennel. "I'll be back soon. Be a good puppy."

"You got lucky with that one," Abby said. "Faith didn't get a wink of sleep last night. She said her puppy peed the bed, chewed a hole in her favorite shirt, and whined half the night. She's dead on her feet."

Noel gave Abby a horrified look then glanced back at Buffy. "You're the best puppy that ever existed. We'll be back."

Abby chuckled, and led the way out of the inn and down the street to the town's coffee shop, Incantation Café.

Hanna Pelsh spotted them and beamed from behind the counter. The morning light streaming through the window illuminated her dark skin, and Noel itched to take more photos of her. Photography was a hobby of Noel's, and Hanna was her favorite model. "Good morning, ladies."

"Morning, Hanna," Noel said. "I need the largest, strongest coffee you have."

She laughed. "Rough morning?"

"You could say that." Noel turned to her sister. "Same?"

"Make mine the largest, strongest mocha you can find," she told Hanna. "I need the sugar."

Hanna's eyebrows rose. "Your morning must be a doozy of a day. Weren't you already in here once this morning?" she asked Abby.

"I was, but unfortunately that round was a bust. You better give us two of those bear claws as well."

"And a couple of coffee cakes," Noel added with a somber nod. "It's one of those days."

Hanna frowned. "Is it that bad?"

The sisters glanced at each other. Then Noel said, "Yes."

"It's not Lincoln, is it?" Hanna asked, referring to their father. Concern radiated from her, and Noel's heart warmed. Hanna was like family, and it felt good to know she loved Lin just as much as the Townsend sisters did.

Noel turned to Abby, realizing it was the first time in days she'd hadn't woken up worrying about him. Up until a few weeks ago, Noel had been the one to take him to all of his chemo appointments, the one who knew what potions and medications he was taking. But since Abby had reclaimed her work shed on the Townsend property, she'd taken over. It just made more sense. She was right there, keeping an eye on him. "Dad's okay, right?"

"Yeah," she said, "He's good, actually. Feeling better. The nausea is under control, and he's not nearly as fatigued."

"Good." Hanna beamed. "So today is just normal suckage, then?"

Abby chuckled as she paid for their breakfast. "Pretty much."

"Have a seat. I'll bring your drinks and pastries out to you," Hanna said.

Noel followed her sister to a table in the far corner near the window.

"Sit. Spill your guts," Abby said, sliding into one of the seats.

"Just like that? You're not even going to let me savor my coffee first?" Noel sat across from her and rested her chin in her hands.

"Better to rip the Band Aid off, don't you think?" The sun streamed in the window, basking her little sister in the soft light. She practically glowed with a quiet happiness. If Noel's camera had been handy, she would've snapped some shots right then and there.

Noel sat back in her chair, really seeing her sister for the first time in years. "You look…"

"Like I need to sleep for a week and spend some time at the salon?" Abby asked with a rueful grin. "I've been burning the candle at both ends trying to finish my holiday orders. If I have to make one more batch of lotion this year, I think I'm going to lose it." Abby was an earth witch who ran a successful business selling magically infused soaps and lotions. Business was booming, and this holiday season had been insanely busy for her. Despite it being the beginning of December, she still had orders to fill… rush orders because the stores had run out. Noel couldn't have been more proud of her little sister.

"No." Noel reached across the table and covered her sister's hand with her own. "You look radiant. Settled. Content. It's really nice." She matched her sister's rueful smile and added, "And really annoying."

Abby shook her head, appearing both amused and exasperated. "Thanks. I think."

"That was definitely a compliment," Noel said as Hanna arrived with their caffeine and pastries.

"Let me know if you need anything else," Hanna said.

"Thanks." Abby squeezed her hand briefly, and the pair shared a bittersweet smile.

Noel felt as if she was on the outside looking in. She shouldn't have. Hanna was her friend as well, but Charlotte, Hanna's sister, had been Abby's best friend. They both had deeply loved Charlotte, and the pain they shared for her loss ran deep. Noel had once had a friendship like the one Charlotte and Abby had shared. Or at least she thought she had. Abby had been her best friend, or at least she was right up until she'd fled town and left everyone behind. Their relationship had fallen apart, and it was only now, over a decade later, that they were even trying to put the pieces back together. Noel feared they'd never be as close as they once were.

"Noel," Abby said, her brows knitted with concern. "*What* is going on? You look like someone stole your Christmas present."

Noel let out a huff of laughter. That was kind of how she'd felt watching Hanna and Abby share their moment. But she wasn't going to tell Abby that. She wasn't proud of how she felt. It was awful to be jealous of a friendship that was so important to her sister. "I'm just having a bad morning."

Hanna gave her a sympathetic pat on the shoulder. "Boy, I know how that goes. Yesterday, I tripped on the curb on my way in and not only ripped the knees out of my favorite jeans, but I fell in a patch of mud and shattered the screen on my brand-new iPhone. Then to top it off, Georgia called in sick and I was all by myself." She shook her head. "I was a mess all day. I sure hope a little sugar, caffeine, and some sister time helps your day recover."

"I'm sure it will," Noel said, taking a sip of her latte.

After Hanna retreated, Abby took a drink of her mocha, sat back in her chair, and waited. Her gaze was so intense that Noel started to feel uncomfortable.

"What?" she asked her sister.

"Something is seriously off. The Noel I know is never shy about what's on her mind unless there's something troubling her. You barely said anything last night except to chastise Dad about the puppy. Today you overslept, something you never do, and you haven't lectured me once about the fact I'm still wearing my work apron. Come on, what gives?"

Noel took a good look at her sister. Abby was right. Noel wasn't herself at all. She was usually up by six every morning, always was particular about the way she dressed even when she just wearing jeans, and while she wasn't always super chatty, she was usually a lot more engaged when she was around her family. She blew out a breath, knowing she had to talk. If she didn't, she was likely to sink deeper into her personal twilight zone. "Drew took me to Eureka yesterday."

Abby blinked, then sat up straighter. "Eureka? Why? A date?"

Another huff of laughter escaped Noel's lips. "Like that would ever happen."

"He likes you," Abby said simply.

"Maybe." Noel tore off a piece of bear claw, but instead of taking a bite, she just set it on the plate and stared pointedly at Abby. "But he's not interested, so let that one go, would you?"

Abby opened her mouth to say something but seemed to think better of it and just nodded instead. "Okay. I will. Why did he take you to Eureka?"

"Law enforcement found a body. They thought it might be Xavier."

Abby let out a loud gasp. When two women at another table turned to stare at the sisters, Abby clamped a hand over her mouth and muttered, "Sorry." She reached out with her other hand, taking Noel's. "Tell me it wasn't him."

"I had to go ID him," Noel said, her voice monotone as if she were in a trance. "Drew drove me to this ugly brick building in downtown Eureka. That one-story, dirt-covered, beige building."

Silence fell between them. Noel stared unseeing out the window, grateful her sister wasn't pushing her to finish. All she could think about was the moment she'd expected to find Xavier beneath that sheet.

One single tear rolled down her cheek. She didn't bother to wipe it away as she turned back to Abby and said, "I was so

angry when he left. I hated him, Abby. What he did to us…
what he's done to Daisy. Some days, on my worst days, I've
wished he was dead."

Abby squeezed her sister's hand, holding on tight. "I'd say
that's a natural reaction. He hurt you. It doesn't mean you
meant it."

"I think I did," Noel choked out. "But I don't mean it now. I
swear I don't."

"Of course you don't."

Noel was shaking and chilled to the bone when she finally
looked her sister in the eyes and said, "It wasn't him."

Wood scraped against wood as Abby pushed her chair back.
She let out a breath she seemed to have been holding and stood
up, pulling Noel to her feet. Noel was momentarily frozen as
her sister's arms came around her.

"You're okay, Noel," Abby whispered. "I promise."

Noel didn't know if it was the sound of her voice or her
sister's embrace, but suddenly her trance broke, and relief and
gratitude rushed through her. Her arms went around Abby,
and the pair of them stood there for a long moment just
holding on to each other.

"It wasn't your fault," Abby said. "None of it was your fault."

Noel pulled back, putting an arm's distance between them.
"How do you know that?"

"Because I know my sister," she said with conviction.

Noel wasn't at all sure that was the case. Abby had been
gone for over a decade. But in that moment, she wanted more
than anything to believe her. She gave her sister a hint of a
smile, and said, "Thank you."

"You're welcome," she said, sounding surprised and a little
off-kilter. But then she returned the smile and sat back down.
"Now, drink your coffee before it gets cold and I have to order
round three."

CHAPTER 9

DREW COULDN'T GET Noel out of his mind. It had been three days since he'd taken her to Eureka. Three days that he'd been making phone calls trying to snag a lead on her ex. So far, he'd turned up nothing. The county sheriff's office had placed the case on the back burner after a domestic altercation had turned into an active manhunt.

He got up from his desk at the station and walked out into the lobby. "Hey, Clarissa, I'm headed down to Incantation Café. Want anything?"

The young redhead stood. "I can go."

"No, no." He shook his head. "I can use the walk."

"Oh. Right." She sat back down, appearing to be slightly disappointed, but said, "Okay. I'm cool. I've got my tea here."

"You're sure you don't want anything?" he asked.

"I'm sure." Then she patted her stomach. "I was craving one of those salted caramel chocolate tortes from A Spoonful of Magic, but I'd better not. You go. I'll stick with my granola bar."

He raised a skeptical eyebrow. "Granola bars are the food industry's cruelest joke."

She laughed. "Don't I know it." Waving a hand toward the door, she added, "Go on, now. I have reports to file."

Drew gave her a two-fingered salute and stepped out into the crisp air. It was the first week of December. The scent of damp earth and redwood trees permeated the air. The skies were blanketed with gray. The winds from the night before had died down, and to him the day was glorious, the perfect winter day. He liked the stillness of it. Peaceful, calm, familiar. He shoved his hands in his trouser pockets and automatically turned down the street toward the coffee shop.

Normally when Drew took his walks around town, he stopped to talk to the establishment owners. Ninety-nine percent of the time, all they did was chitchat, but every now and then, he caught wind of suspicious activity that led him to investigate. More than once he'd caught on soon enough that he'd stopped a crime before it even started. Usually those cases were teenagers pushing boundaries, but not always. Sometimes they were more nefarious intentions, such as setting up meth houses or illegal grow houses. Keating Hollow was tucked away just enough so that criminals sometimes decided it was the perfect spot for hiding out. They'd be right except for the fact that Keating Hollow was a community of witches who looked out for their own.

Today, though, Drew had other things—other people—on his mind. He crossed the street and walked by the Keating Hollow Inn, peeking in the front window. Noel was at the reception desk, but she was on the phone, rapidly typing something into the computer. He watched as she picked up a mug of coffee, went to take a sip, and frowned when she found the cup empty. She made a face, abandoned the cup, and went back to typing.

Drew smiled to himself and kept on walking. He'd intended to go straight to the café, but when he reached A Spoonful of Magic, the enchanted nutcrackers in the window caught his attention. They were busy decorating witch-shaped cookies with Mrs. Claus outfits and holiday lights. He chuckled. Only in Keating Hollow.

The door swung open, and Shannon stepped out onto the sidewalk. "Officer Baker," she cooed as she placed a hand on his chest. "Don't you look handsome this fine December morning."

The deputy had a strong desire to step back. He'd known Shannon forever. The redheaded beauty had changed a lot since high school. Back then they hadn't run in the same circles. And from what he remembered, she hadn't been the nicest person. But she'd matured over the last decade, as they all had, and she'd turned into someone who was kind and generous and someone he found charming... when she wasn't blatantly coming on to him. He'd made the mistake of taking her out on a date not long ago, and even though he'd made it clear he didn't think they were a good fit, she seemed determined to change his mind.

"Thank you, Shannon," he said. "You look lovely as always."

Her lips curved into a seductive little smile that he was sure worked on every other man on the planet. What was his problem anyway? Shannon was beautiful, smart, and sexy. And available. It would be so much easier if he was just attracted to her. Unfortunately, his mind kept wandering to the woman with the empty coffee cup.

"Thank you," she said. "Care to come in for some of Miss Maple's special cocoa? I just made up a fresh batch."

"Um, I was headed to the café for some coffee. I should probably—"

"Nonsense," she said, already tugging him inside the chocolate shop. "I've got fresh coffee, too. I'll take care of you."

There was no doubt about that, Drew thought. But his mind wasn't working fast enough to gracefully extract himself from her clutches, so he let her pull him inside. The scent of rich chocolate engulfed him, and his mouth started to water. "This place is dangerous, Shannon," he said, eyeing the salted caramel chocolate torte Clarissa had mentioned. "Do you and Miss Maple add some sort of addictive ingredient to get us all hooked on this stuff?"

She chuckled. "Only if you think cocoa beans are addictive."

"No doubt they are if you've had your hands on them."

An amused gleam lit Shannon's dark gaze. "My hands *are* magic. Want to test them out sometime?"

Heat crawled up Drew's neck. He'd really stepped in it that time, hadn't he? "I think I'll just get a couple of mochas and a piece of the salted caramel chocolate torte for now."

"I see." Her expression clouded with irritation just before she gave him a bright smile. "Two mochas, huh? Got a coffee date?"

"No, just picking up something for a friend." He took a step back and eyed the cookies in the window, pretending interest so he didn't have to keep talking to Shannon. He knew from experience she'd just keep flirting and trying to talk her way into a date. It's how he'd ended up taking her to dinner last month. He wasn't going to fall for it again.

"Did you want a box of cookies to go with this?" she asked from behind the counter.

Drew glanced over at her. She was standing perfectly still as a ribbon wrapped itself around a festive holiday box beside her. A few feet to the left, two stainless steel frothing pitchers floated in the air while the milk for the mochas was being steamed.

"Sure. A dozen?" he said. He'd leave them with Noel for her guests.

Shannon waved a hand, sending the cookies into a tissue-lined box. She moved to the register, hit a few buttons, and held out her hand for his credit card. While he paid, the mochas finished making themselves and the two boxes flew into a holiday bag. By the time he signed the receipt, his purchases were lined up on the counter.

"Thank you, Shannon. You saved me a trip down to Incantation Café," he said.

She just shrugged, clearly annoyed by his brushoff. "I'm sure you'll end up down there later today. You always do."

"I guess you're right." He grabbed the bag and the tray holding the mochas and headed for the door.

"She's not over her ex. You know that, right?" Shannon said.

Drew glanced back at her. "Who isn't over her ex?"

Shannon rolled her pretty brown eyes. "Who do you think? Noel Townsend. The woman you want to date but can't seem to muster the courage to ask out."

An automatic denial formed on Drew's lips as he shook his head.

"Don't bother trying to deny it, Deputy Baker. It's obvious to everyone with eyes."

He let out an irritated sigh. Clay had called him out about his feelings for Noel a few days ago, and now Shannon. Only they were wrong. He didn't want to date Noel. He just wanted to be her friend. "You don't know what you're talking about."

"If you say so." She shrugged and turned her attention to the display case, where she started rearranging the already perfectly arranged confections.

Drew stepped out onto the cobbled sidewalk, ignoring the voice in his head that kept saying he was full of utter crap. Friends. Right. That's why he hadn't been able to stop thinking about her. He tightened his hold on the tray of mochas and strode down the street to the Keating Hollow Inn.

The door chimed as he stepped inside. Warmth engulfed him, and he instantly felt more at ease in Noel's cheerful space. The only thing that could have made it better was if Noel had actually been there. But the lobby was empty, and no one was manning the check-in desk. He placed the bag of goodies and mochas on the counter and pressed the bell next to the computer.

He waited patiently. And after a minute or two, he pressed the bell again.

Nothing.

Strange, he thought. Noel was never far from the desk, and if she was, she always left a note or a number or put Alec in charge while she was away. He glanced up the stairs, wondering if she was dealing with some sort of guest issue. If so, no doubt she'd be down eventually. He unwrapped the Christmas-inspired witch cookies and placed the open box on the counter. Then he grabbed one of her Post Its and wrote, *Happy Yule. Merry Christmas. Happy Solstice.* He attached the Post It to the counter and moved to tap the bell again, but stilled when he heard a high-pitched yell, followed by a crash that came from her residence.

"Noel!" he called out, instantly on alert and worried about her safety. He rushed behind the counter while simultaneously reaching for his stun gun. Crime in Keating Hollow was rare, and Deputy Baker didn't even carry a firearm. But a stun gun was necessary. If a witch got out of hand, it was just about the only thing that could neutralize their magic. There was something about the electric current that temporarily zapped them of their powers.

Pressing his shoulder against the door, Drew called Noel's name again.

"Help!" she shouted back.

There was no hesitation. He burst into her apartment. A trail of clothes had been strewn across the living room, and a glass of milk had shattered on the floor.

"Noel! Where are you?" he barked, moving quickly to the first open bedroom door. The twin bed and overabundance of stuffed animals meant it belonged to Daisy.

"In the kitchen! Hurry!"

Drew sprinted to the kitchen door, adrenaline pumping through his veins. Holding the stun gun out, ready to strike, he kicked the door in. It flew open and slammed into the wall.

"What the hell was that?" she asked from under the sink. Water covered the tile floor, and Noel was drenched from head to toe. She glanced up at him, her eyes going wide when she saw his stun gun. "Cripes, Drew. Put that thing away. Are you trying to electrocute someone?"

"I thought... never mind." Drew made sure the safety was on and placed his weapon on the island counter. "Plumbing issues?"

"What makes you ask that?" she asked dryly. "I just walked in and found water everywhere. It's spewing from this line, but I can't stop it."

He kneeled down, spotting the problem immediately. One of the fittings had come loose from the supply line, and water was spewing from the broken connection. "Is there a reason why you didn't just shut the valve off?"

"Gee, why didn't I think of that?" She held up the water valve knob. "It came off in my hand."

"Oh," he said with a chuckle, nudging her out of the way. Magic rushed to his palms as he reached for the leaking plumbing line. "I've got this."

"What do you think you're going to do?" she asked as she stood. "Nothing's going to help until—"

"There." Drew got to his feet and reached for a hand towel on the counter. The water was contained, but the plumbing still needed to be repaired. "If you have a wrench handy, I can get this done in a few minutes."

"How did you—" She shook her head as recognition lit in her gaze. "Water witch. Right. But… how is it *still* contained? You don't seem to be wielding your magic right this moment."

Drew grinned at her. "I have really good stamina."

"Is that right?" she asked with a laugh. "Cocky much?"

"Confident," he said with a wink. "Wrench?"

Her lips curved into a tiny, amused smile. "Sure, Mr. Fix-it. Coming right up."

He couldn't take his eyes off her as she crossed the kitchen to a small utility closet. Her wet jeans were pasted to her backside, and her shirt was see-through enough that he could make out the outline of her lacy bra. He couldn't help but imagine what it would be like to strip her out of her clothes and run his hands over her as he dried her off.

"Drew?" she asked, standing in front of the closet with a small tool box in her hands.

"Huh?" He blinked, heat crawling up his neck for the second time that morning. Son of a… what was wrong with him? If he was determined to remain just friends, daydreaming about her naked body wasn't going to help.

"Is this what you need?" She held up a crescent wrench.

He blew out a breath and nodded. "That should do it."

"Good, because it's the only one I have." Noel crossed the room and handed it to him. Her fingers grazed his, and an actual spark of electricity crackled between them.

Neither one of them broke the connection.

Drew stared down at their hands, watching the magic shimmer over their fingers.

Noel let out a small, nervous laugh. "Well, that was unexpected."

"You think so?" he asked, raising his gaze to hers.

The smile vanished from her face as she searched his eyes. "Yes... and no."

He knew he should pull his hand back and break their connection. But he just couldn't. Her light air magic was warm and inviting. It made him imagine sitting out on the beach with her in his lap while they watched the sun set over the Pacific.

Noel pulled her hand back, breaking the magical connection. His insides turned cold just as he heard the sound of water gushing behind him.

"Crap!" Noel grimaced. "I'll go shut the main line off."

"I've got it." Drew cursed himself. He'd been showing off when he'd insisted he had great stamina. His magic had been acting as a dam, keeping the water from spraying from the loosened line. It was never meant to hold forever. Switching his focus to Noel had sped up the inevitable. He ducked back under the sink and held one hand over the leaking pipe. The water instantly stopped flowing. With the other hand, he grabbed the loose bolt that had fallen to the bottom of the cabinet and said, "I need the water valve knob."

Noel placed it in his hand, and in no time at all, Drew had the bolts, valve, and waterline reconnected. He got to his feet, turned the faucet on, and waited to see if there were any new leaks. It was just a precaution, really, because he could feel it in his bones that the water was contained and flowing correctly.

"Thank you," Noel said from behind him.

"You're welcome." He turned the water off and leaned against the counter, his arms folded over his chest. "Glad to help."

Her expression turned soft as she swept her gaze over him.

There was a tenderness about her that he so rarely saw, it made his heart ache just a little.

"You got a little wet," she said.

She was right. He was pretty much drenched from the knees down. "It's fine. But you..." He gestured to her. "You might want to change before any guests arrive."

Noel glanced down at herself and let out a small gasp as she covered her chest with both arms. "Why didn't you tell me I was indecent?"

"Indecent?" He chuckled. "Not exactly."

"Close enough." She hurried out of the kitchen, and as soon as she stepped into the other room, she let out another cry. "Buffy!"

Drew followed her and couldn't help the bark of laughter when he spotted her on her knees, butt in the air, as she reached under the couch. Buffy darted out with a sock in her mouth and ran straight into Daisy's room.

"Dammit!" Noel sat up on her knees and glanced around at the clothes strewn across her floor. "So much for thinking the laundry was done." She held up a milk-stained sundress. "Buffy had a field day while I was dealing with the kitchen flood."

Drew calmly walked over to Noel, took the dress from her, and offered a hand up. She blew a blond lock out of her face and let him pull her to her feet. He squeezed her hand and said, "You go get changed. I'll start cleaning up."

"I can't let you do that, Drew," she said as she reached for a Daisy-sized T-shirt.

He took that from her, too. "Of course you can. I offered. Besides, you're indecent, remember?"

"Crap." She closed her eyes as she covered her chest again. "Okay, but only because you're insisting."

He snorted out a huff of laughter. "To be clear, you look sexy as hell all drenched like you've just been the star of a wet

T-shirt contest. So I'm not insisting on anything, but I imagine you'll feel a lot more comfortable once you're in some dry clothes."

Noel stared at him for a few seconds, then shook her head and muttered something about mixed signals.

He pretended to not hear her and proceeded to pick up the clothes that Buffy had dragged into the living room. After placing them on the washing machine in the utility room off the kitchen, he grabbed some cleaning supplies and went to work on cleaning up the broken glass and spilled milk.

By the time Noel returned with Buffy in hand, Drew was mopping up the last of the water in the kitchen.

"Drew." She tilted her head to the side and studied him, wonder radiating from her wide eyes. "You didn't have to do all of this."

He placed the mop in the bucket and turned to her, slightly overwhelmed by her beauty. It was rare to see her so unguarded. Drew knew he was responsible for putting that look on her face, and he wanted to do it again and again and again. "I know. I wanted to."

"Well... thank you. Who knows what would've happened if you hadn't shown up." She glanced down at Buffy. "This one likely would've destroyed Daisy's entire wardrobe while I completely flooded the kitchen."

Drew washed his hands and said, "You'd have figured it out. You always do."

"Maybe. But it sure doesn't hurt to have help every once in a while."

He mimed tipping his hat. "Happy to oblige, ma'am."

The bell chimed, indicating a guest had arrived. "Oops." Noel handed Drew the puppy and said, "I'll be right back. Don't go anywhere."

Drew watched her slip out of the residence and then

glanced down at Buffy. "You're one lucky little dog, you know that? If you'd done that at my place, you'd be in the dog house for sure."

The puppy wagged her tail.

He chuckled and got down on the floor to play with her. He found a small ball rolling around under the coffee table and proceeded to teach her how to play fetch.

CHAPTER 10

"HAPPY ANNIVERSARY. ENJOY YOUR STAY," Noel called after the two young women as they headed to their room. They'd been married in Keating Hollow the year before and were back to celebrate their first anniversary.

They both glowed as they smiled back at her. Noel put a hand over her heart, soaking in their joy. *So sweet*, she thought, and then she wondered if she'd ever experience that kind of happiness again.

Not if you don't even try, the voice in her head chastised.

She let out a frustrated sigh. The problem with letting herself love again was the inevitable pain when things went south. And in her experience, they always did. There was a time in her younger days when she'd believed life could be different. But then Abby had fled not only Keating Hollow, but also the relationships that were most important to her, leaving Noel to put the pieces back together. And then Noel's marriage had ultimately ended up just like her father's. Despite appearing to be happy, both her mother and her husband had left town and never looked back.

In her experience, everyone always left. It wasn't something she could risk again.

Her gaze landed on the Mrs. Claus witch cookies and the two coffee cups from A Spoon Full of Magic. *Drew.* Damn him. Why did he have to be such a good guy? No matter what she told herself or how hard she tried to not have feelings for him, he went and did things like fixing her plumbing, cleaning up the mess, and bringing her cookies and Miss Maple's wicked mocha lattes.

The man was pure evil in all the right ways.

She grabbed the coffee cups and headed back into her residence. Pausing just inside the door, she placed the drinks on the side table and watched as Drew scratched behind Buffy's ear and praised her for being a smart girl. A smile tugged at her lips. Cripes on a cracker that man was cute. And sexy, too.

He tossed a small ball across the length of the living room for Buffy and cheered her on as she chased it. She promptly brought it back to him and dropped it in his hand then sat and waited patiently for the next toss.

"I can't believe you taught that dog to fetch in the house," Noel said.

Drew threw the ball again. "She's maybe five pounds. How destructive can she be?"

"You saw the clothes incident, right? Daisy is out a pair of socks, a sundress, and a T-shirt."

"Collateral damage." He rose from the floor and walked over to her. "At least her play time will wear her out. I bet she crashes and sleeps the afternoon away."

"Perfect," Noel said with a mock grimace. "Then she'll be well rested and tromping all over the bed, wanting to play at midnight."

He raised one eyebrow. "The dog sleeps in your bed? I thought she had a crate."

"She does, but that lasted all of about ten seconds before I caved."

He glanced down at Buffy. "Lucky dog."

Noel laughed. "Yeah, well. She's living a charmed life so far."

"Like I said, lucky dog." His gaze shifted past her, and he reached for the coffee cups. "I see you found the mochas."

Noel took them out of his hands and started moving toward the kitchen. "Too bad they turned cold while you were cleaning up for me." She strode into the kitchen and popped them in the microwave.

Drew followed, unable to stay away now that she was back.

She turned and stared at him, her expression searching.

He took a step closer and brushed a lock of hair behind her ear. "What is it, Noel?"

She sucked in a breath and met his gaze. "You can't keep being so nice to me, Drew. I'm going to get too used to it. You shouldn't be bringing me cookies and mochas. Especially not ones from A Spoonful of Magic. Shannon is probably spitting nails."

"There's nothing going on with Shannon," he said with a sigh. "In case you missed it, Shannon is not my girlfriend. Nor will she ever be."

"I know, but—"

"There's no but about it, Noel," Drew said cupping her cheeks with both hands. "I took her on one date. One awful date that was so uncomfortable I was checking my watch before our drinks even arrived. Understand?"

"Yes," she whispered, her gaze shifting to his mouth.

Her fresh citrus scent washed over him, and all his reasons for remaining just friends fled. His heart pounded against his ribcage as he leaned in closer, wanting her more than he'd ever wanted anyone before. The rest of the world faded away, and the only thing that mattered was kissing her.

"Drew," she said breathlessly. "What are you doing?"

"This." He closed the distance between them, gently brushing his lips over hers.

Her eyes fluttered closed, and she leaned into him, her arms circling his waist.

The kiss was tender and perfect, but Drew needed more, needed her. He buried one hand in her thick golden locks and deepened the kiss, tasting her for the second time in his life. And this time was so much better.

Holy hell, was it better. Every nerve in his body sparked to life, and he felt like a suffocating man who was finally breathing again. He bowed her back, one hand supporting her while he held her close. The kiss seemed to last forever and at the same time was over all too soon.

Their lips parted, and both of them were breathing heavily. With her hair cascading behind her, Drew thought Noel had never been more beautiful.

"Drew?" she asked, pressing her palm lightly against his chest.

"Yeah." He continued to gaze at her in wonder, already wanting more of her.

"You have to let me up. It's a half-day at school, and I'm going to need to go get Daisy soon."

"Oh, sure." Drew righted her and made sure she was steady on her feet before he let go. Her hands lingered on his shoulders, and Drew pulled her against him once more. Her soft curves fit perfectly against him, and he wondered what he'd been thinking all those years. "Kiss me again, Noel."

Her fingers dug into his flesh as she pressed up on tiptoe and did as he asked. A shudder of pleasure reverberated from his very core, making him want to scoop her up and carry her the ten feet to her bedroom. Before he could contemplate that last thought, Noel broke the kiss and gently pressed her palm to Drew's chest. "I really do have to go get Daisy."

"Right." He backed up, giving her the space she needed, and ran a hand through his thick hair. Son of... what had he just done? He glanced at the contented expression on her face and started to hate himself. How long would it be before he talked himself out of pursuing a relationship with her?

She smiled up at him and leaned in, kissing him on the cheek. "Thank you, Drew. I don't know what I would've done without you today."

Her sweet voice soothed his doubts. It didn't matter what his inner voice tried to tell him. He knew he wasn't going to be able to step away from whatever was going on between them. Not now. Not after feeling her soft and pliant in his arms. "No need to thank me." He reached past her, opened her microwave, and handed her one of the mochas. "Here. Don't want you to miss out on this."

Her eyes twinkled as she took a sip. A low, appreciative moan escaped her lips as she closed her eyes. "This is delicious."

So are you, he thought. "Go. I'll get Buffy settled in her crate before I head back to work."

"Buffy... oh no. Where is she now?" Noel ran out of the kitchen, mocha in hand. When Drew stepped into the living room, the dog was laying in the middle of the floor, chewing on the ball. Noel turned to him. "You did this. Earlier today, she wanted nothing to do with any of her toys." She shook her head in disbelief. "I owe you. Big time."

"No, you—"

"Yes, I do," she said, cutting him off. "Let me take you to dinner. Tomorrow night. Seven. Daisy and Buffy have a sleepover date with Olive and her golden retriever puppy,

Endora. We can go to Woodlines. I heard they have a fabulous new chef."

Drew did not want their first date to be Noel taking him out. He wanted to be the one to spoil her, not the other way around. But he sure wasn't going to turn her down. "Tomorrow night is perfect."

"Good." She flashed him one more radiant smile, then rushed out of the residence.

Drew glanced down at Buffy. She was happily gnawing away at the ball, content as could be. "Buffy," he said.

The dog immediately disregarded the ball and gave him her full attention.

"Ready to go out?"

She jumped to her feet and followed him to Noel's small yard. She promptly did her business and then followed him back in. "Time to find your crate."

The dog lowered her tail and gave him the saddest puppy dog look he'd ever seen.

"You're not pulling that business on me, little girl," he said, scooping her up. "You can't stay out here unattended. Your rep precedes you."

The crate didn't seem to be in Daisy's room, so he headed to Noel's. The moment he stepped through the threshold, her subtle citrus scent engulfed him. Her furniture was dark, antique wood with just a hint of scroll work in the headboard of her bed. Everything else was clean lines. It was perfect for her. Hard angles with a hint of softness.

He walked over to the crate at the end of her bed, checked to make sure she had clean water, and then placed Buffy inside. She stared up at him with that same pathetic puppy dog stare. "Don't look at me like that. I'm not the one who chewed holes in Daisy's clothes."

At the sound of his voice, she turned her head away as if annoyed but then circled three times and curled up into a ball.

"Good, Buffy," he said quickly and closed the gate to the crate.

The longer Drew stood in her room, the more intense Noel's citrus scent became. It only made him want to sit in the armchair in the corner and wait for her to come home so he could kiss her again.

He just might've, too, if his phone hadn't gone off. "Drew Baker," he said into the phone.

"Deputy Baker," Clarissa said, her voice a little shaky. "I think you need to get back here."

"Back to the office?" Dread materialized in his chest and settled in his gut. "What's wrong?"

"I'm not sure, but the Humboldt County sheriff wants to talk with you."

"I'm on my way."

CHAPTER 11

DREW STRODE into the small satellite office. Clarissa, who'd been sitting on the edge of her seat, jumped up with a small stack of messages for him.

He handed her the chocolate caramel torte he'd picked up at A Spoon Full of Magic and said, "Save those messages for later. I don't want to keep the sheriff waiting."

She shoved a piece of paper at him again. "I think you'll want to see this one now."

Her insistence made him pause. He took the piece of paper and glanced down.

Xavier Anderson is officially the lead suspect in the John Doe case. He's been spotted twice. Once at Pacific Cove Boat Rentals and once at the Moon River Inn. Word is the sheriff wants you to stay out of it. He's not happy about the background check flagged from the Keating Hollow satellite office. C.

"Got it." He handed the note back to Clarissa, grateful she'd given him a heads up. The sheriff was likely pissed he'd been poking around a case that wasn't assigned to him. Before he walked into his office, he added, "Thanks."

"You're welcome, boss," Clarissa said, already pulling the torte box out of the bag.

He squared his shoulders, braced himself for the impending ass-chewing, and walked into his office. "Sheriff Barnes. What a surprise. What brings you all the way out here to my corner of the world?"

The gray-haired, heavy-set man was seated in Drew's chair behind his desk, scribbling something on a legal pad.

"Sit down, Baker," he barked.

Drew did as he was told and waited for his superior to finish whatever he was writing. Finally, the sheriff scribbled what looked like a signature and stuffed his pen back into his uniform pocket. When he looked up he said, "What have you found out about Xavier Anderson?"

Drew shook his head. "Nothing."

"Don't play games with me, Baker. I know you've already started investigating. I need to know everything you know."

Drew was certain that if he admitted he'd been butting in on a case that was out of his jurisdiction that there could be professional consequences, but since his boss already knew he'd started digging, there really wasn't a choice in the matter. "I ran a preliminary background check on him three days ago. Nothing came up. At least not anything in the three years since he left Keating Hollow. Since then, I've learned from the rumor mill that he's been spotted twice over in Eureka in the last week. No one seems to know where he's staying or where he'll show up next."

The sheriff's expression remained completely neutral. "And *why* were you looking into Mr. Anderson? Did his ex-wife ask you to?"

"What?" Drew frowned. "No."

"You just did it on your own? Why?"

Drew shifted uncomfortably, knowing he was showing his

nerves. "I knew the department was short-handed, so I took it upon myself to see if there were any obvious leads or threads that would help find Mr. Anderson."

The sheriff nodded as if that answer was acceptable. Then he cleared his throat. "I heard you accompanied Ms. Townsend to the morgue. Is there a relationship there I need to know about?"

Son of a... What was he going to tell the sheriff? That he'd just been making out with her? That he had a date with her tomorrow night that he was hoping would turn into something more than a couple of drinks and a really good steak? "Noel Townsend and I have been friends for a long time," he said carefully. "When I delivered the news that her ex-husband might be deceased, I didn't feel comfortable with her driving into Eureka by herself."

"So you're friends." The sheriff wasn't giving anything away, and Drew had no idea where this line of questioning was headed.

"Yes. Friends." And that was the stone-cold truth. A least in that very moment.

"Good. Keep it that way." The sheriff stood and handed over a piece of paper with his official letterhead at the top. Below, he'd handwritten a directive authorizing Drew to take the reins in tracking down Xavier Anderson.

Drew read the directive twice to be sure he was reading it correctly. The order was in direct conflict with the information Clarissa had given him just before he'd walked into the office. Of course, whatever she'd heard was just rumor. The sheriff surely wouldn't put him on a case if he was pissed he'd already looked into it, would he? Drew blinked and glanced back up at the sheriff. "Why are you giving this to me?"

Barnes hesitated for a moment before continuing. Then he

cleared his throat. "I need someone on the outside looking into this."

Warning bells went off in Drew's head. "You mean there could be an internal affairs issue?"

Barnes sat back down in the chair, suddenly looking tired. "Honestly, Baker, I don't know. But there have been too many unanswered questions, and records seem to have gone missing. I just need to let someone else take a look at this for right now. And since we can't move forward until we find this guy, I need you to get started right away. He's the only connection we have at the moment," he said. "You have a relationship with the ex-wife of our person of interest. If they're in contact, you'll be able to intercept. Plus, your office is quiet. You have another deputy who can take care of this town while you're investigating. But most of all, I trust you to go the distance to see this investigation through to the end."

"Noel isn't in contact with her ex. I can guarantee that," Drew said, somewhere between annoyed and pissed off that his superior was implying Noel was somehow still caught up with the asshole who'd abandoned her.

"Fine. But he might still get in touch. If he does, you'll be there." The sheriff strode over to the door. "Keep this one close to the vest. Without knowing what's going on internally, I'd prefer my guys didn't get wind that I handed this off to you. Got it?"

"Got it," Drew said, a little stunned. He was just one guy. If there were shady cops participating in a cover up, he had his work cut out for him. And Drew couldn't blame the sheriff for being suspicious. If the sheriff's staff weren't any better than the county officials he and Noel had dealt with at the coroner's office, the environment was ripe with opportunities for payoffs and incompetence.

"Good. Keep me updated on any new developments. The

case file is in your top drawer." Without waiting for an answer, the sheriff strode out and closed the door behind him.

Drew sat in his chair, temporarily stunned. The county sheriff had never handed off a case to him before. It was true that Keating Hollow was a quiet town with rarely any crime to speak of, so he certainly had time. But he wasn't a detective. Something didn't add up. He got to his feet, moved over to his desk, and yanked the top drawer open. The unmarked folder was right where Barnes had said it would be.

Sitting in his chair, Drew pulled the thin file out of the drawer and flipped it open to find only one page. It read:

Subject: Xavier Anderson – Person of interest in a suspected murder.

Mission: Find Mr. Anderson and bring him in for questioning. Where has he been the last three years; who has he been in contact with; and what has he been doing?

Notes: Anderson has ghosted and is currently in the wind; no paper trail since March 2015. There have been possible sightings in Eureka in December of 2018. Possible internal interference in the case. Strongly suspect magic is involved in his disappearance.

DREW STARED at the last line. They suspected magic. No wonder they'd tossed the case to him. As far as he knew, he and Putzner were the only two witches on staff in the county. And Putzner wasn't interested in doing anything other than writing parking tickets. It's why Drew was in charge of the satellite office.

All right then, Drew thought as he fired up his computer. This was what he'd wanted in the first place; to find Noel's ex and give her some closure. Now he'd just been given the green light.

So why did he feel so uneasy about it?

He ran a hand over his head and logged into the case number listed on the sheet of paper the sheriff had left him. Xavier Anderson's face instantly appeared on his screen. The two sightings Clarissa had warned him about were listed. Then there was nothing until his disappearance three years ago. He scrolled down and frowned. The first record of Xavier Anderson's existence was one month before he married Noel.

"What?" he said out loud to no one. That was impossible. A thorough background check run by the department on a missing person would include voter registration, traffic violations, arrest records, previous addresses, and any government identification such as a driver's license or passport or state ID. It could also include names of family members, any military service, and even credit reports. There wasn't anything more listed here than he'd found in a basic public records search.

Xavier Anderson hadn't existed before he'd married Noel, and he'd ceased to exist after he disappeared. Something wasn't right in Andersonville. Xavier had a current driver's license and credit cards. They should've shown up on this report. Was he using fake aliases and stolen credit card numbers? If so, why had he reused Xavier Anderson if he was trying to stay under the radar? He was going to have to get the credit card and license numbers from the evidence room down at the station. How was he going to do that without tipping someone off? He had no idea.

Drew printed out the flimsy records and added them to the file he'd already started on Xavier.

A knock sounded on his door.

"Come in."

Clarissa poked her head in. "Everything okay? What happened?"

"It's fine." He gave her a reassuring smile. "The sheriff just wants me to take over an investigation for him." He held up his file. "Can you give Putzner a call and let him know I'm headed out of town? He'll need to cover if anything comes up. Tell him I'll let him know when I get back."

"Sure, boss. Anything else I can do for you?" she asked as she opened the door and stepped inside.

He started to refuse but then thought better of it. "Yes. Any chance you have any connections down at the evidence and property department in Eureka?"

"Sure. I have a friend who works there. What do you need?" She flipped open a notebook and clicked the end of her pen.

"The credit card and driver's license number for Xavier Townsend. His wallet was found on the John Doe, and they aren't showing up on the background check."

She frowned. "That's unusual. You think they're fake?"

"Maybe. But I can't be sure until I run them down," Drew said.

She made a note then glanced up at him. "Any reason why you need me to ask my friend to do this? Seems like it would already be in his file."

"That's exactly why I need your help. It's not there. And just between you and me, something smells to high heaven. I want to keep this quiet until I figure it out."

"You got it, boss. Anything else?"

"Not right now." He fished his keys out of his pocket. "Just call Putzner. That should be enough torture for one day."

She snorted out a laugh. "Don't worry about me. I know exactly how to handle him."

He just bet she did. Clarissa was sweet as pie when people were kind to her and treated her with respect. But the minute they turned on her, she shut them down hard and fast with just a couple of words. It was fascinating, really.

Drew followed her out into the lobby. Before he could even

reach the front door, she was already on the phone notifying Putzner.

"Listen, Pauly, cut the attitude," she said. "It's in your job description to be on call when necessary. So unless you're resigning—oh, no? Okay then. I'll let you know if any calls come in."

She was still dressing him down when Drew stepped out onto the cobbled sidewalk. He glanced across at the inn, his lips tingling with the memory of kissing Noel in her kitchen. His feet automatically started moving in that direction. It wasn't until he stepped off the curb that he caught himself. No, he couldn't just barge in on her. Daisy was there, and he had a job to do. He'd talk to her tomorrow. On their date. Their first date.

Damn, after the encounter they'd had, he didn't know if he could wait the twenty-seven hours to see her again.

CHAPTER 12

NOEL SAT at her dad's dinner table, nibbling on her blackberry pie. Her dad had called and invited her and Daisy for dinner not long after she'd picked Daisy up from school. She hadn't realized that when she'd said yes, it meant she was going to be ambushed by Abby.

"Come on, Noel," her sister whined. "You have to. It's girls' night."

"Abby," Noel said with a sigh. "I have to be up early. I can't be your second in your crazy golf cart races with Wanda."

"But she's already recruited Hanna. If you don't go, I'm going to have to kidnap Faith, and the last time she rode with me, she lost her lunch." Abby pressed her hand to her stomach, clearly still queasy over the situation. "I don't think doing donuts in the mud is her thing."

Noel couldn't help the laugh that burst from her lips. "Donuts? Are you insane, Abs? You're going to kill yourself on that thing."

Her sister just shrugged. "Don't be so dramatic. You just have no idea how much fun it is since you haven't given it a try. As Wanda says, it's the most fun you can have with your clothes on. I promise you, you won't regret it. Dad already offered to keep an eye on Daisy. You guys can just stay here for the night. Isn't Alec on duty tonight at the inn?"

"Yes," she said, shaking her head in exasperation. There was no winning this argument with her sister. The fact was, she wasn't even sure she wanted to. Oh, she was in no rush to tool around in the freezing cold air, but she was enjoying this side of her sister. This animated, excited version of Abby was the Abby of their youth. The one she'd been before they'd lost Charlotte. Noel couldn't shut her down just because she wanted to stay inside where it was warm and drink hot cocoa.

"So you're in?" she asked, her eyebrows raised.

"I'm in. But we're going to go check on Yvette first," Noel added. "She's been a little... *off* lately, and I want to make sure she's okay."

"Sure!" Abby popped up off her chair and grabbed her phone. "Just let me tell Wanda we're on."

Noel watched her do a crazy little dance and couldn't help but be amused. For far too long, Abby had walked around in a cloud of sadness, and now she was this crazy golf-cart-racing fool who exuded happiness. It was pretty wonderful.

"Mommy!" Daisy called as she ran in from outside. Buffy ran in after her, leaving a trail of mud in her wake.

"Daisy! Don't let Buffy track mud all over the house. Pick her up. Now."

Daisy skidded to a stop and barely managed to snag Buffy before she got mud all over the area rug. "Mom!" her daughter cried again, a wobble in her voice. "Hurry, it's Grandpa."

Fear ran like ice in Noel's veins. "Dad?" she called, already moving toward the back door. When she didn't hear him respond, she turned to Daisy. "What happened, baby? Where's Grandpa?"

"This way." She darted back out the door, Buffy still in her hands.

Noel raced after Daisy, who led her straight to her father's gardening shed. Daisy held Buffy with one hand and pointed inside. "He fell."

"Dad?" Noel rushed in to find her father sitting on the floor, trying to haul himself up. "Don't move, Dad. You're hurt."

He glanced over at Noel and grimaced. "It's just a twisted ankle. If you can help me up, I can use those old crutches to get around."

She swept her gaze over him, scanning his body for any other obvious injuries. Other than his ankle and being pale and too thin, he looked like he was all right. She placed a soft hand on his shoulder. "Dad, stop. Just stay right there, and I'll be back in a minute."

"I just need a hand, Noel," he said through gritted teeth.

"You need an x-ray and some pain killers." Noel turned to Daisy. "Keep an eye on your grandpa. Make sure he doesn't try to stand on that leg. I'll be back in two shakes."

Noel spun around and nearly ran smack into Abby.

"What happened?" she asked.

"He fell. Twisted his ankle. I'm going to get your golf cart so we can get him out of here."

Without hesitation, Abby pulled the key out of her pocket and handed it to her sister. "Go. I'll get him something for the pain."

Noel nodded and ran across the property, tears threatening to blur her vision. "Dammit!" She angrily brushed the tears aside. This wasn't the time for a breakdown. Besides, it was just an ankle. She was sure once they got him looked at, he'd be just fine.

The only problem was she couldn't shake the image of him

looking so weak and helpless there on the floor of the shed. Her dad was her hero, her rock, the person she admired and leaned on the most. She didn't want to think about his mortality or what their world would be like if they lost him. Noel knew she was being dramatic. It was just an ankle... this time. But he was still undergoing chemo treatments. An injury like this likely wouldn't heal quickly, and reduced mobility was a concern.

She jumped into the driver's seat of the golf cart and wiped her tears. Her father needed her to be strong, and she would not let him see her shaken. Noel turned the key, flipped on the lights, and whipped the cart around the side of the house. Luckily, there was a clear trail that led to the shed, and when she pulled to a stop beside the building, Abby already had their father up and hobbling to the door. He had his arm around Abby's shoulder while she bared the brunt of his weight. Luckily, he didn't have far to go.

"I can just use the crutches," Lin said again, scowling as he leaned into Abby. "You girls don't need to treat me like an invalid. And I don't need to see a healer. It's just a sprain."

Despite her father's stubborn agitation, Noel felt the weight of fear lift off her. If he was being surly about their fussing, that meant he wasn't in too bad of shape.

"We're not treating you like an invalid, dad. We're treating you like a man who, at best, has sprained his ankle or, at worst, broke something. So yes, you do need to see a doctor. You don't want to make it worse, do you?" Abby asked.

Their dad tried to put weight on his injured foot and grunted.

"See?" Abby said, rolling her eyes.

"I thought you said that potion was supposed to be for pain," he said pointedly to Abby. "I'm sure all I need to do is rest for a few days."

"Dad," Noel said, shaking her head. "Abby's potions aren't miracle drugs. And they aren't a substitute for medical treatment. You know that."

Lin and Abby finally reached the golf cart. She helped him get settled in the front passenger seat, while Daisy and Abby and Buffy slid in behind them.

"Onward," Abby ordered.

Noel didn't hesitate. She stepped on the pedal, and despite Lin's protests, she hauled him straight to the urgent care clinic on Main Street.

CHAPTER 13

"WAIT HERE," Noel said, as she pulled into the spot right in front of the clinic.

"Do I have a choice?" her father grumbled.

"No," Abby and Noel said at the same time.

Abby grinned at her sister and took Daisy's hand. "Come on, little one. Sit up front with Grandpa and keep an eye on him."

Daisy crawled into the driver's seat with Buffy on her lap. "It's okay, Grandpa. I'm here."

Noel glanced between her daughter and her father and felt as if her heart was going to explode with emotion.

Abby clutched her hand to her chest and let out a little moan. "Geez. Is that the cutest thing you've ever seen, or what?"

"Definitely the cutest." Noel pulled the glass door open and followed Abby in.

"Abby! Noel!" Gerry Whipple said from behind the reception desk. The older witch and her husband had been the town healers for over twenty years. "What brings you in this evening?"

"Our dad fell and hurt his ankle," Noel said. "He's outside in the golf cart."

"Oh dear." She pressed a button on the phone and spoke into the intercom. "Martin, we need your assistance, please."

"On my way," her husband said through the line.

"He's just in the back catching up on some files. He'll be here shortly." Gerry rose from her chair, produced a wheel chair from the closet, and waited by the door for her husband.

The older gentleman strode out of the back, wearing a white lab coat. His salt-and-pepper hair was more salt than pepper, and he had a kind smile for the Townsend sisters when he spotted them. "Good evening ladies. You just caught us before we were going to close up shop. What seems to be the problem?"

"It's our dad." Abby pointed at the golf cart through the window.

"Twisted ankle," Gerry said. "I need you to help me get him into the wheelchair so we can check him out."

He nodded, and the pair of them went outside to help Lin into the chair. When they wheeled him in, Lin was quiet and paler than ever. Noel sucked in a breath, fear racing up her spine. He did not look good.

"Just wait here, ladies. Let us check him out, and then we'll come get you," Martin said.

Noel glanced out the window at her daughter still sitting in the cart. "Is it okay if we bring the puppy into the waiting room? Daisy's out there with her, but—"

Gerry placed a soft hand on Noel's forearm. "It's fine, dear."

"Thank you." Noel opened the door and waved for Daisy to come inside. Her daughter ran in, her teeth chattering from the cold. She was wearing a fleece, but the temperature had dropped and must've chilled her to the bone. A shiver ran through Noel as her adrenaline wore off, and she waved a hand and imagined a rippling fire in the middle of the office. The air in the room instantly warmed.

Daisy let out a sigh of relief, snuggled her face against Buffy's warm body, and said, "That's better."

"It sure is." Abby sat down in one of the chairs and grabbed a magazine. "You should keep that trick handy for when we go out later."

Noel frowned at her sister. "Are you insane? We can't go out later. Dad is hurt, and I have Daisy."

"Dad is going to be just fine," Abby said, flipping a page in her magazine. "And I'm sure Faith won't mind hanging with Daisy. The two puppies can visit."

"Yay!" Daisy said. "Buffy misses her sister."

Noel scowled. She hated it when her sister voiced her plans without asking Noel about them first. All it did was get Daisy excited, and then Noel had to be the bad guy when she said no. "You don't even know what Faith is doing tonight. You can't just—"

"Faith is taking Xena to puppy school, and then she's coming out to the house for a visit. She'll probably be there by the time we get dad home."

"So then take Faith on your golf cart races," Noel said, crossing her arms over her chest.

Abby gave her sister a horrified look. "Didn't you hear me earlier when I said Faith couldn't stomach the donuts? Oh, no. I'm not doing that again. Faith is only good for leisurely rides along the river. No races."

"Abby—"

"Good news, ladies," Gerry said, striding back into the

reception area. "Your dad just has a sprain. He's a little weak, so we're prescribing a couple of energy potions—"

"What kind of energy potions?" Noel asked as she stood. "Abby's already got him on one of her concoctions. Most of the other ones we've tried haven't worked in the past."

"Oh, dear," Gerry said, making a note. "Maybe Abby should come back so we can go over what has worked and what hasn't."

Abby shook her head. "Noel would know better than I would. They tried quite a few things before I moved home."

"You're sure?" Noel asked her, surprised her earth witch sister was willing to let her handle this one. Abby knew a lot more about potions than Noel did.

"Yeah. You know what I'm giving him now and what he tried before. I'll wait here with my favorite niece." Abby squeezed Daisy's hand.

"Okay." Noel waved to her daughter and followed Gerry into the back to an exam room where Martin Whipple was fitting her dad's foot into an air cast.

"Stay off it as much as possible the next few days. The air cast should do the trick, but when you're ready to move to regular shoes, use an elastic bandage for support."

"All right," her father said. He was sitting on the end of an exam table, and some of the color had come back into his cheeks.

When Healer Whipple was done, he rose and headed for the door. "I'm going to go get that bandage and some anti-inflammatory medication for you. I'll be right back."

"Noel," Gerry said. "I wonder if I can see you for a moment?"

"Um, sure." She stood and glanced back at her father. "I'll be just a minute."

"I'm fine, Noel. Go on," he said, waving a hand. "Don't look so worried. I'm in a clinic, for goodness sake."

"All right, all right. So, sue a girl for being worried, why don't you?" she muttered as she followed Gerry into another exam room.

"Have a seat," Gerry said.

Noel glanced around the sterile room. The only place to sit was on the exam table. "Um, Gerry, is this about my dad?"

She shook her head. "No, dear. I want to take a look at you. Your energy seems low, and I want to make sure everything's humming along as it should."

"I don't—"

"Just humor me, okay?"

"Sure." Noel climbed up onto the exam table as her nerves took over. "It must be something terrible if you can just sense that something is off."

The healer looked up at her with kind eyes and gave her a reassuring smile. "Not necessarily. I'm gifted at reading energy levels, and yours are dangerously low. Have you been over doing it? Feeling run down? Sore throat, maybe? Burning the candle at both ends?"

Noel shrugged. "No sore throat. As for the rest, it's no more than usual. I'm a single mom who runs an inn and is keeping an eye on her dad as he battles cancer. I guess you could say my stress is probably higher than normal."

Gerry nodded as she took Noel's blood pressure. "It's a little high," she said when she was done. She listened to Noel's heart, took her temperature, checked her glands, and then sat back. "Well, you certainly seem to be in good health, but you do appear to be rundown. Have you been getting enough sleep?"

"Not really," Noel said. "It's been a little stressful, and I've had a bit of insomnia. Plus, we have the new puppy to care for."

Gerry nodded. "Then you could definitely use some more rest. So, here's what I want you to do; I'm going to suggest a vitamin booster pack, and I also want you to make room in your schedule for some down time. Do something fun that helps you blow off steam. You can't be worrying all the time. That kind of stress wears on you until it wears you out. Okay? Vitamin pack, rest, and destress, got it?"

"I guess so."

Gerry scribbled the name of the vitamin pack onto a prescription pad and handed it to Noel. "I'm willing to bet if you take these vitamins, give yourself a half-hour a day just for you, and go out and have some fun, your energy will be back to normal in no time."

Right, Noel thought. The idea that she had to schedule personal time for herself just made her feel more stressed. But she took the prescription and nodded anyway. Gerry was just trying to help.

Gerry led her back to her dad's exam room, where she and Lin waited for Martin Whipple to return.

Her dad turned to her. "What was that about?"

"Gerry just wants me to start taking some vitamins." She showed the script to him. "She says my energy levels are low. I'm probably just working too hard."

"There's no doubt about that," Lin said. "You've always burned the candle at both ends, but you can't keep that up for forever."

She pretty much had to, didn't she? No one else was going to run her inn or pay the bills. But she didn't say anything to her father. He knew all too well the pressures of raising a family on his own. She glanced at his air cast. "Did they get an x-ray?"

Her father nodded. "I told you it was just a sprain."

"So you did," she said and moved to sit next to him. "You know we were just worried about you, right?"

Lin put his arm around his daughter and pulled her in for a sideways hug. "I know, sweetheart."

"It's just better to be safe than sorry. With everything that's going on, we need to make sure we're keeping you as healthy as possible."

Her father was quiet for a moment. Then he turned and looked her in the eye. His gray gaze searched hers as he asked, "Is everything okay with you, Noel?"

She blinked. "Of course. Why do you ask?"

He let out a small chuckle. "Why wouldn't I? The healer just told you your energy is low, and you weren't even here for a checkup, which means she was concerned enough she gave you an impromptu exam. Plus, you're wound up so tight, I'm surprised you haven't started spinning."

"Dad." Noel sighed. "Don't turn this around on me. I was just concerned about your ankle. What if you'd have broken it? Were you just going to wait it out?"

"That's not what I'm talking about." He brushed her hair out of her eyes. "I'm talking about the heaviness you carry around with you everywhere you go."

"It's just a stressful time," she said, turning her head to look away from him. Why did she feel like a fifteen-year-old all over again? "I'm not the one being a pain in the ass about medical treatments."

He laughed. "You got me there."

The sound of his amusement was contagious, and she looked back at him, smiling. "So, you're admitting it then?"

"I admit to nothing," he said with a wink. But then he sobered. "Listen, Noel, I heard about your visit to Eureka."

She stiffened. "Did Abby tell you that?"

He gave her a strange, searching look. "No. Clay did. He didn't realize I didn't know."

So it was *Abby,* Noel thought. She should've known her sister couldn't keep a confidence. She was the same old Abby, blabbing everyone's business. Of course, Noel hadn't exactly told her sister not to say anything. And it was perfectly natural for her to talk to her fiancé about it.

"Why didn't you tell us?" her dad asked, concern in his tone. "That must've been really hard, thinking you were going to identify Xavier."

Tears filled her eyes, and she hated herself for it. She'd vowed never to cry over him again, and yet here she was with her dad, blubbering like a fool. "I just… didn't want to talk about it."

Lin nodded. "That's understandable. But you know, talking about it helps."

Noel let out a tsk of disbelief. "Really, Dad? How often did you talk about Mom after she left?"

"To you girls? Only when you brought her up," he said. "I didn't want you to hate her in case she actually showed back up. But to my therapist? A lot. I had plenty of issues to work through. I imagine you do, too."

"I'm fine," Noel said.

Lin laughed. "Like father like daughter, right Noel?"

"What's that supposed to mean?"

"Both of us are as stubborn as a mule, that's all. No one would ever call either of us pushovers." He winked and bumped her shoulder with his.

She wanted to be mad, to blow off this conversation, but maybe he had a point. It wasn't like she didn't know she was being stubborn. "A counselor, huh? Did it help? Did you ever stop resenting Mom for leaving?"

"Not really." He placed his hand over hers and squeezed her fingers. "But I did learn how to trust again."

Trust. There it was. The six-hundred-pound elephant in the room.

"And how to love again," he said softly.

A sob got caught in her throat.

"Listen, baby. Maybe we should've had this conversation months ago. But you have to understand that most people aren't like your mother and Xavier. They don't willingly leave families they love. Your mother..." He shook his head. "I don't think she was ever happy. To be honest, I don't think even *she* knew what she wanted. Maybe we married too young. Or maybe she felt trapped."

"Or maybe she was just a selfish witch," Noel said.

"Maybe," Lin said, giving her a sad nod. "But the point is, we don't know, and we aren't likely to *ever* know. Would knowing really make a difference in the outcome anyway? She wasn't here. We survived, thrived even, and our lives are filled with love. I just want you to have everything you've ever wanted; the family, the 2.5 kids, and even the dog. Nothing good ever comes from closing ourselves off."

"You already took care of the dog part," she said, narrowing her eyes at him.

He chuckled. "So I did."

They were silent for a moment. Then Noel said, "If I keep my barriers up, maybe I won't get everything I want, but I won't get hurt either."

"Are you sure about that?" he asked.

No. The word popped into her mind without her even giving it any thought. She didn't want to be alone, didn't want to lose whatever had started between her and Drew. She just didn't know if she could handle it if someone else she loved left her again.

"Without trust, we're not whole, my sweet girl," Lin said, squeezing her fingers again. "I just want you to be happy. To live your life your way and without fear."

"I do live my life my way." She was sure of that, at least.

"Yes. You do." Lin patted her knee as the healers returned. "Just think over what I said. See if any of it fits."

"Sure, Dad." Of course, his words fit. Her dad always could see past her defenses. The only problem was she didn't know if she was ready to let go of the past.

CHAPTER 14

DREW PULLED into the parking lot of the Moon River Inn. The rundown motel was south of Eureka and sat on the banks of the Eel River. Drew climbed out of his SUV and scanned the mostly empty parking lot. Not exactly a happening place, was it? That was both good and bad. Xavier wouldn't have been hard to remember. But if there wasn't anyone around to notice him, then Drew would be up a creek without any witnesses.

The sun was already low in the sky when Drew walked into the motel's office. Stale smoke combined with a faint mildew smell hung in the air, and he wondered when they'd last opened a window or thought to spray a little air freshener.

"Need a room, handsome?" an audacious redhead said from behind the counter. She was wearing a low-cut blouse, her ample cleavage spilling out onto the counter as she leaned forward. Drew imagined most men had a hard time not staring at such a display, but he was still trying to process the beehive hairdo and the fake eyelashes that were so long they looked like she had a spider attached to each eyeball. *Interesting look*, he thought.

"Actually, I'm looking for someone," Drew said, pulling out Xavier's picture.

"Aren't we all," the woman said, puckering her lips as she swept her gaze down the length of Drew's body.

Drew felt his skin start to crawl and had to force himself to stay put. His reaction surprised him, and he chalked it up to a sixth sense warning him to tread carefully. The woman was certainly over the top, but so far she hadn't done anything too outrageous. He placed the printout of Xavier's picture on the counter and asked, "Have you seen this man?"

"Today?" she asked as she picked up a pack of cigarettes.

"In the last week or so."

She pulled a cigarette out of the pack and rolled it between two fingers. "Who's asking?"

"Deputy Sheriff Baker, ma'am." He slid a card across the counter to her. "I'm just trying to get in touch with him."

"Is he in trouble?" She placed the unlit cigarette between her lips and fiddled with a lighter but made no move to light it.

"Not that I'm aware of," Drew said. No wonder the place smelled of smoke. Under California law, smoking wasn't permitted indoors, but Drew was willing to bet the woman would light up just as soon as he left the building.

She glanced at the printout again, appearing to study it. When she looked up, she just shrugged. "I don't recall seeing anyone who looks like that. But then again, this place is pretty busy."

Drew glanced around the office and peered outside. There were only two other cars besides his in the parking lot. "Do you get a lot of overnights here?"

"Yeah," she said with an enthusiastic nod that pulled a few locks loose from her beehive. "I imagine we'll be getting an after-dinner rush here shortly."

Drew doubted that. The motel wasn't right off the highway.

It was unlikely they got a lot of drop-ins who overnighted on the way up and down the coast. "Okay. Thanks for your help. But if you do see him, can you give me a call?"

She glanced at the card again. Then she swept her gaze over him one last time as she licked her bottom lip. "Sure, Deputy Sheriff Baker. It would be my *pleasure.*"

He gave her a short nod and strode out of the office and back to his SUV. He climbed into his vehicle, but instead of firing the engine right away, he eyed the woman inside the office. Night was falling, and thanks to the office lights, he could see right inside and watch her every move.

She picked up his card, appeared to study it, then ripped it in half and tossed it into a nearby garbage can. A moment later, she lit her cigarette. He wasn't surprised. Despite her obvious interest in him physically, she hadn't had one bit of interest in helping him find Xavier. He had a feeling she was hiding something or protecting someone. Xavier maybe? Would Noel's ex really go from a class act like Noel to someone who looked ready to perform on a Vegas stage?

Drew wasn't quite sure what to make of her. All he knew was that getting information out of her was a lost cause.

He turned the engine over and pulled out onto the two-lane highway, heading for the diner he'd passed on the way to the inn. There weren't a lot of businesses nearby, so it was reasonable to assume that if Xavier had stayed at the hotel, maybe some of the nearby residents had seen him.

The gravel crunched under his tires in the Pies, Pies, and More Pies parking lot. A neon sign flashed over the entrance that read, *Blackberry.* A few seconds later, it changed to *Apple.* His mouth watered as he thought about digging into a fresh-from-the-oven apple pie.

With Xavier's picture in his pocket, he entered the modest establishment and sat at the counter. The place looked like it had last been updated in the eighties. The booths were orange vinyl with laminate tables. The linoleum was so worn there were actual holes wearing through to the subfloor. But the round-faced waitress behind the counter had a genuine smile as she set a menu and a ceramic mug in front of him and asked, "Coffee?"

"Yes, please. Thank you, Sally," he said after reading her nametag.

Her eyes were bright and inviting as she filled his cup and asked, "Cream and sugar?"

"Black is fine." He flipped the menu over, spotted the apple pie a la mode he coveted and pointed to it. "Just get me a slice of this, and I'll be forever in your debt."

She chuckled. "You got it, champ. Anything else?"

"That should do it for now." He passed the menu back to her and said, "Thanks."

While Sally bustled around behind the counter, Drew turned and scanned the joint. It was surprisingly busy for a place that was a little bit off the beaten path. A handful of young families were dining on burgers and fries; two older gentlemen were in a booth off to the side, playing cards; and a half-dozen teenagers, drinking sodas and sharing a giant plate of nachos, filled a table near the back. Then there were all the singles, hanging out and eating pie. He had to laugh. He fit right in.

"Here you go," Sally said, sliding his pie in front of him.

"Thanks." He picked up his fork and took a bite. He closed his eyes and let out a little moan of pleasure as the mixture of cold ice cream and warm pie hit his tongue. "This is delicious."

"That's what they all say." She winked at him and moved on to refill some coffee mugs. Sally had the same warmth with all her customers as she did with him. It was obvious she liked people, and Drew was sure that if she'd met Xavier, she'd remember him.

He took his time finishing his pie, and when Sally returned to refill his mug, he said, "Can I ask you a few questions?"

She leaned an elbow on the counter, cocked her head to the side, and said, "Shoot."

There was no suspicion with this one. Good. He was in luck. "I'm trying to track someone down. He was staying at the inn down the road a week or so ago, and I'm guessing if he wanted to eat, he likely stopped in here."

Sally nodded. "Probably. Everyone seems to make it here sooner or later."

"I don't doubt it. That apple pie was the best in recent memory." He took the scanned photo out of his pocket and slid it over to her. "Can you remember seeing him around here?"

She took one glance at the photo and nodded. "Sure. That's Victor. He was here with another guy. Xavier, I think."

"Victor?" Drew wrote the name down in his notebook. "You're sure that's what he was calling himself?"

She laughed. "I have no idea what *he* called himself, but that's what his friend called him." Her eyebrows knit together as she contemplated what he'd said. "Why? Was he using an assumed identity? Was he using stolen credit cards?"

"Stolen credit cards?" Drew shrugged. "It's possible I guess, but credit card fraud isn't why I'm looking for him."

"I swear to the goddess, if we get charges back because of those two douches, I'm going to pitch a freakin' fit." Her eyes flashed with anger as she slammed her fist down on the counter.

"Hey!" One of the old guys called out. "Keep it down, would ya? I'm trying to concentrate here."

Sally ignored him and stared straight at Drew, her

vivacious personality suddenly heated. "I knew those guys were trouble. I just couldn't put my finger on why."

Drew raised both eyebrows. "Can you elaborate on why you were suspicious of them?"

She let out a huff of laughter. "Sure. The one guy, not this one," she said, pointing to the picture in front of her, "was a complete jerk. He kept calling me honey, and normally that wouldn't bother me, but when it comes with a leer and an ass-grab, it's more than I can take."

Son of a... what the hell was Xavier doing hanging out with that jackass? Drew had known the man when he'd lived in Keating Hollow, and Xavier had never been anything but a gentleman as far as Drew knew. Why was he associating with a guy like that?

"Victor," she said, pointing at the picture again, "told the douche to cut it out, but his friend just laughed like it was a big ole joke. At least Victor was a decent tipper."

Drew cleared his throat. "Did they say anything about why they were in town?"

She frowned and rubbed her forehead, concentrating. "Something about a job with a fishing boat, I think. They were usually headed to Yachtsmen's Harbor."

"Perfect." Drew made another note. "When was the last time you saw them?"

She shrugged. "Maybe a week ago?"

Drew nodded. "That's helpful. Anything else you remember about them? Anything they talked about or did?"

She held her hands palms up in an I-don't-know gesture. "I listen to a lot of people. I think the only reason I remembered them is because that Xavier guy was a complete a-hole."

"And Victor?" he asked, knowing that when she said Xavier she was talking about the John Doe. "How was he?"

"Fine I guess, except for the company he kept."

Drew shut his notebook and handed her his business card. "Thank you, Sally. I'm Deputy Sheriff Baker, and if you see this guy again, I'd appreciate it if you'd call me as soon as possible."

"Is he in trouble?" she asked, biting her lower lip.

"No." Drew shook his head. "We just need to talk to him." He threw a twenty on the counter, knowing it was about four times as much as his bill. "Thank you for your time. You've been very helpful."

CHAPTER 15

NOEL PLACED a cup of hot cocoa and a tray of cookies on the end table and fluffed a pillow before tucking it under her dad's knee. "Here's your energy potion and the supplements Healer Whipple recommended. Faith is on her way with a stew she cooked up today, so you'll have something to eat for the rest of the week. When she gets here, we can play a game. What do you think about Monopoly?"

"Noel." Her father covered her hand with his. "Relax. I'm fine."

"Of course you are," she said, handing him his mug of cocoa. "Drink this before it gets cold."

Lincoln Townsend glanced down at the mug then at the smiley face cookies Noel had decorated after dinner and shook his head. "What am I? Five?"

"Dad, I'm just—"

"You're hovering, Noel." He placed the mug back on the side table. "I'm going to have to insist that you get out of my hair. Go take that silly golf cart out with your sister. You two are driving me crazy."

Noel placed her fisted hands on her hips and shook her head. "I'm not going anywhere. Who's going to be here if you need something?"

"Daisy will be here." Her dad gave her a withering glare. "Now go on before I call Deputy Baker and have him haul your butt out of here."

Abby snickered.

Noel cast an irritated glance at her sister. "You're being unreasonable, Dad."

"No, you are." He fished his phone out of his pocket. "You have two minutes to get out of here, or I'm calling the law and turning you in for trespassing."

"Drew isn't going to haul us out of our family home," Noel insisted, mortified at the idea of Drew having to deal with something as silly as escorting her out of her dad's house.

"You sure about that?" He tapped on the screen. "Let's find out."

"Dad!" Noel grabbed for his phone, but he swiftly moved it out of her reach.

"Oh, look, it's already ringing." He pressed the phone to his ear.

"Stop! Okay, okay. I'll let Abby take me out on her golf cart. Just don't call Drew."

He gave her a self-satisfied smile, tapped the screen, and then shoved the phone back into his pocket.

"But we're going to wait until Faith gets here," Noel said stubbornly. She wasn't going to leave her six-year-old in charge of her father. Besides, what if Daisy got into some kind of trouble while her dad was laid up in the recliner?

"Fine. But wait for her over in the kitchen. I just want to watch the Duke take out these bad guys." He gestured to the television, where the opening credits were rolling for one of his John Wayne movies.

"You win, Dad," Noel said, chuckling to herself. He was right. She was hovering and worrying needlessly. Considering how feisty he was being, he obviously felt just fine. "Abby and I will be over there plotting how to annoy you next."

"No doubt you will." He picked up the cocoa and took a sip. Then he pointed the remote at the television and turned the sound up to an almost deafening level.

Abby slid off her bar stool and gestured for Noel to follow her. Noel glanced at Daisy playing with her dog in the middle of the living room, seemingly oblivious to the noise, and eagerly followed her sister into one of the bedrooms.

"What's up?" Noel asked her.

"I got a text from Faith. She's on her way with provisions for Dad. She and Xena are going to spend the night, so she said she'd love it if Daisy and Buffy could stay, too. She thinks it will be good for Xena to spend some time with a well-behaved puppy."

Noel raised one eyebrow. "Buffy isn't well behaved. Not yet anyway. She's learning, but she still chews things she's not supposed to. And she's already had an accident since we got back from the healer."

"I don't think you can understand until you've spent some time with Xena. She's literally the devil dog. You're just gonna have to take pity on Faith and let her have this one."

Noel narrowed her eyes at her sister. "Is this all some elaborate plan so I'll stay out later with you and do donuts in the mud?"

Abby laughed. "No. I'd come up with something way better than that. Something like maybe inviting Clay and Drew to the party."

"Stop," Noel said, shaking her head, but she couldn't help the smile that claimed her lips.

"Oh... uh-oh, what's this about?" Abby waved her hand in

front of her sister. "You're smiling, and it has everything to do with the town deputy."

"Maybe." Noel fidgeted with the hem of her shirt. "We have a date tomorrow night."

"What?" Abby squealed and grabbed her sister's hands. "You have a date with Drew? How did that happen?"

"He came by the inn today and helped me with a plumbing situation. I'm taking him to dinner as a thank you."

"Plumbing situation?" Abby eyed her suspiciously. "That isn't a euphemism, is it?"

"No!" Noel laughed. "Come on, Abs. You know me better than that. Or at least you used to."

"Of course I do. When we were kids, you were always the cautious one. And now you're even worse." She crossed the room and rummaged through the closet. When she finally found what she was looking for, she spun around, holding two wine bottles in her hands, and said, "Ah-ha!"

"What are these doing in here?" Noel took one of the bottles and read the label. Her eyebrows rose in surprise. "These are special reserve from that great winery down in Calistoga. Where did you get these?"

"I have my evil ways." She grinned. "Actually, they bought some candles from me for their shop in a rush. I might have over-delivered, and they sent me these as a thank you."

"But why are they in the closet?"

"Because, my dear sister, they needed to be stored somewhere cool and out of the sunlight."

Noel studied the wine bottles again, then the closet, and then she started laughing.

"What are you cackling about?" Abby demanded.

"You hid these in here so no one would find them. No one like Clair, perhaps?" she asked, referring to their dad's longtime girlfriend. "She's been known to enjoy her wine... especially really good red wine."

Abby got a sheepish expression on her face. "Okay, maybe. The winery sent it here because this is my business return address, and it showed up late in the day on a night she was cooking for Dad. I just... I put it in here and then promptly forgot about it."

Noel laughed again. "Of course you did."

"Okay, you caught me. Whatever." Abby strode to the door. "But you should be thanking me, because without this, we'd be stuck drinking hot cocoa. And not the fun kind." She jerked her head. "Come on. We have a golf cart race to win."

"CAN WE JUST MAKE ONE STOP?" Noel asked as Abby steered the cart onto the golf cart path along the magical river that ran through the town.

"We already have booze, Noel," Abby said, holding up a plastic cup of wine. "I can't think of anything else we might need."

Noel chuckled. "No, it's not that. I want to check on Yvette. She's been really off lately and I'm not sure she's doing okay."

Abby glanced over at Noel, her eyebrows pinched in concern. "You know what? You're right. She's been really tense the last few times I saw her. Do you think she and Isaac are having issues?"

Noel gazed up at the full moon and sighed. "I hope not. Isaac has been really good to this family. I'd hate to have to beat the crap out of him for mistreating my sister."

"You and me both," Abby said and made the turn onto Main Street. It was a chilly December evening, and the town had rolled up the carpet for the evening. The only places that were still open were the two restaurants and the Townsend Brewery. Judging by the number of cars parked on the street, it didn't appear that any of them were all that busy.

Abby turned right off the main road and in no time, they pulled to a stop in front of a tidy, two-story Victorian. Light poured from the house, and two cars sat in the driveway.

"Looks like they're home," Noel said as they strolled up the walkway.

Abby rang the doorbell and wrapped her arms around her body. "Brr. Is it colder here? Suddenly I'm freezing."

"It's forty-one degrees, Abby. I told you it was too cold for golf cart races," Noel said, rolling her eyes.

"It wasn't this cold when we were on the cart. I swear, this house is in some sort of winter vortex."

The door swung open and Yvette stood in the threshold, her eyes red and puffy as if she'd been crying. Her chestnut hair was tied up in a messy ponytail, and she had a coffee stain on her white shirt.

"Vette?" Noel asked, alarmed by her appearance. She was a complete wreck. "What's wrong? What happened?"

Yvette glanced over her shoulder and shook her head. "I can't talk now."

Isaac appeared just behind her with a duffel bag in his hand. He was dressed in slacks and a steel-blue, button-down shirt. His thick dark hair was freshly cut and his jaw clean-shaven. Tall, and broad shouldered, the man looked like he'd just stepped off the pages of a cologne ad.

"Where are you going?" Yvette asked him. "You can't leave now. We were in the middle of a discussion."

"No, we weren't. You were accusing me of lying while I was trying to explain where I've been the last two nights. And you know what? I don't have the energy for this. I'm going to go stay with Jake for a few days."

"Isaac!" she shouted as he strode to his car. "What the hell are you doing?"

"Leaving," he said and jumped into a brand-new BMW.

"When did he get that?" Noel whispered to Abby.

"No idea. Last I saw, he was driving a Toyota."

"If you're leaving then don't bother coming back, you bastard!" Yvette yelled as the car sped down the street. She let out a tiny little sob and then spun around and disappeared into the house.

Noel and Abby glanced at each other, and without a word they followed her inside. They found Yvette slumped in a chair at her kitchen table, an unopened bottle of wine sitting in front of her.

"Want me to open that for you?" Abby asked, gesturing to the wine.

Yvette tilted her head up, tears rolling down her cheeks. "I —I think I'm gonna need something str—stronger."

"You got it." Noel moved to the freezer on the other side of the kitchen and pulled out a bottle of Gray Goose. Without missing a beat, she poured Yvette a shot then proceeded to rummage around in the fridge for some mixers.

Yvette downed the vodka and poured herself another one before she said, "There's ginger beer in the door."

"Perfect." Noel gathered the ingredients for Moscow Mules while Abby held Yvette's hand.

"What's going on, Vette?" Abby asked her. "I know things haven't been one hundred percent lately, but what is it? Another woman?"

Fat tears streamed down Yvette's face as she shrugged. "I don't know for sure." She closed her eyes and sucked in a shaky breath, trying to get her emotions under control. "I just know that he's lying to me about something. He didn't come home until almost two in the morning last night. The night before that it was midnight."

"Where did he say he was?" Noel asked as she sliced a lime.

"At the office." Another sob got caught in her throat as she added, "But I called there yesterday and—" She paused to collect herself. When she spoke again, her voice was barely audible. "They said he'd already left. That was at seven."

"Oh, honey." Abby wrapped her arms around her sister, pulling her in close as Yvette continued to cry. "I'm so sorry. What did he say when you asked him about it?"

"He said he was at a dinner meeting. But it's not true," she said, her voice muffled. "I have access to the business card. There aren't any charges. He's the boss, he always pays."

Noel brought a pitcher of the Moscow Mules over to the table and poured each of them a glass. Abby's gaze met hers, and the two stared at each other, neither knowing how to navigate this crisis.

"Here." Noel set a glass in front of each of them. She knew it wasn't the most mature response to an impending breakup, but in that moment, there didn't appear to be anything else to do. "Drink this. Then we're going to clean you up and take you out. We have a golf cart race to win."

Abby flashed Yvette a small smile and nodded encouragement.

"I don't want to go anywhere," Yvette said through sniffles.

"We're not going to leave you here to wallow," Abby said gently. "Come on, Vette. Let's just go for a ride and get some fresh air. It will do you good to get out of here for a bit."

Yvette lifted her head and glanced at Noel. "You'll make her bring me back if I want to just come home?"

Noel stifled a chuckle. "Of course, Yvette. I've got your back."

"Hey!" Abby exclaimed. "What are you two implying?"

"I think you're getting a bad rep when it comes to that golf cart," Noel said with a shrug. "Races, donuts... what's next? A souped-up engine?"

"Well..." Abby started.

"You didn't!" Yvette turned to Abby, her eyes wide with surprise. "Are you insane?"

"I have to beat Wanda somehow!" She threw up her hands. "Have you seen the way she gloats? She's even keeping a scorecard in her cart and rubs it in my face every time I see her. I need to get back on top just so I don't have to hear it anymore. I swear, if I didn't love her so much, I'd have to spike her wine with silencing potion."

"Abby, seriously?" Yvette said. "Silencing potion?"

"She's kidding," Noel grabbed a thermos out of Yvette's cabinet. She held it up. "Can't go unless we have our libations."

"You stock the cart," Abby said to Noel. "I'm going to take Yvette upstairs and get her cleaned up a little. We'll be down in two minutes flat."

Noel watched Abby lead Yvette from the room. She'd been in Yvette's shoes three years ago, confused, angry, and hurt. The familiar ache of loss echoed in her soul, and she prayed Isaac and her sister could work it out. They'd been happy not too long ago. There was no telling what had happened between them, but for her sister's sake, she hoped whatever it was could be fixed. Until then, she was going to do everything in her power to make sure Yvette knew she wasn't alone and that her sisters would be there for her... no matter what.

CHAPTER 16

Wanda's cart flashed with purple lights as she idled at the makeshift starting line near the edge of the woods. She tapped her breaks twice, indicating that it was time to start.

"I'll get to the line when I'm good and ready," Abby said and took a big gulp of Moscow Mule. "She thinks she's so cute with her purple lights and Prince blaring from her surround sound. But you know what I have?"

Noel laughed at her. Abby had supposedly brought the extra alcohol for Yvette, but she'd had her fair share and it was starting to show. "What's that, Abs?"

Abby flipped a switch. The lights came on, bathing them in a pink glow. She grinned and hit a button on her iPhone. Natalie Cole belted from the surround sound, singing about her pink Cadillac. "You know the only thing that would make this better?"

"If I were driving?" Noel asked, taking the booze thermos from her sister.

"Very funny," she said dryly. "The only thing that would make it better is—"

"If the cart itself were pink," Yvette said, grabbing the booze from Noel.

"Exactly!" Abby high-fived Yvette and started to climb into the driver's seat, only she missed the step and ended up slipping in the wet grass.

"Okay, that's it. I'm driving," Noel said, sliding over behind the wheel.

"Oh, heck no!" Abby pushed her out of the way and jumped into her spot. "I've been waiting for forever to beat the pants off Wanda. I'm not backing down now."

The cart jerked forward, and both Noel and Yvette let out a cry of surprise.

"Okay, seriously now," Noel said, holding on tightly to the rail. "Abby, are you sure you're okay to drive?"

"Yep. The grass is just slippery. I've got this." She inched up to the starting line right next to Wanda's cart.

Wanda turned her music down and indicated for Abby to do the same.

"What is it, Wanda? Ready for a serious butt-whipping?" Abby taunted.

"Butt-whipping?" Hanna said with a laugh. "What are we, twelve?"

"It would appear so," Noel said as she waved a greeting to Hanna and Wanda. Hanna waved back, but Wanda was focused on Abby.

"You're going down... again, Townsend. Ready to eat dirt?" Wanda taunted back and added, "That makes four to zero in my favor. I can't wait to add another check mark to my tally."

"We'll just see about that." Abby tightened her grip on the steering wheel. "Let's get this done. To the river and back? First one over the line wins bragging rights and two dozen Decadent Delights from A Spoonful of Magic."

Noel and Yvette shared a glance. Decadent Delights were

Miss Maple's special creation, handmade by her and infused with her earth magic. They were the definition of to-die-for.

"Let's do it," Wanda said and handed a horn to Hanna. "When the horn blows, you better be on your toes."

"Hit it!" Abby said.

Hanna held the horn in the air and said, "Ready, set, go!"

The piercing sound filled the air, and both golf carts lurched forward. Noel and Yvette cheered and started chanting, "Go, go, go, go!"

Wanda turned Prince back on, and the volume drowned out their cries of support.

"Oh, no she didn't." Noel raised her hand, held her thumb and forefinger an inch apart, and whispered, "Volume."

Prince's voice faded to a dull roar, and Noel cackled as Wanda flipped her off.

"That's hilarious, Noel, but if you haven't noticed, they're ahead by half a cart length," Abby said, sitting on the edge of the seat and leaning forward as if that would make the cart go faster.

"I thought you said you added a booster to this thing," Noel said.

"I did, but I have to use it at the end, otherwise it drains too much of the battery. And even then, it's not going to make up that much distance."

"I have an idea," Yvette said from the back seat. She leaned forward, poking her head between them. "Noel can use her air magic to give us a boost."

"Yvette! That's cheating," Noel said with a bark of laughter. "We can't do that."

"The hell we can't," Abby said, bouncing in her seat. "Go on, Noel, give us a boost."

"Do it! Do it! Do it!" Yvette chanted. The huge grin on her face as she gave herself over to the moment was such a stark contrast to the way they'd found her, and Noel just couldn't say no. She'd make the golf cart grow wings and fly if it meant she could prolong this moment of joy for her sister.

"All right. I'm on it." Noel twisted around and climbed into the back of the cart with Yvette. She pointed to her empty seat and gestured for Yvette to take her place. "Go on. Be Abby's new wingman."

Yvette let out a *whoop* and pulled herself over the seat. She and Abby continued to chant, "Do it! Do it! Do it!"

Chuckling to herself, Noel faced the back of the golf cart, held her hands straight out, and said, "Blow."

Wind began to build behind the cart, gathering like a giant ball of invisible energy. When the ball was practically bursting with energy, Noel turned back around and rested her arms on the seat in front of her.

"Go, go, go!" Yvette cried as Abby steered the cart and made the U-turn at the edge of the river.

Wanda and Hanna were a full length ahead of them by then. Noel just smiled, thinking about the look on Wanda's face when she saw them sail right past her. It was going to be epic.

As soon as Abby had the cart through the turn and headed straight for the finish line, Noel cried, "Release!"

The energy in the ball of wind crackled and flew toward the back bumper of the cart, shooting it forward with an impressive force.

The three sisters pumped their fists in the air as they passed Hanna and Wanda, overtaking them by an entire cart length.

Noel heard Wanda curse, and she chuckled to herself. Now that they'd opened the door to using magic, there was no telling what the other two would try. But she highly doubted that Wanda's fire magic or Hanna's water magic would be much help in this situation.

Just as she started to contemplate how they might use their magic to their advantage, heavy rain started to pelt the cart.

"What the heck? Abby exclaimed. "It wasn't supposed to rain tonight."

"It's just raining on us!" Yvette called over the pounding raindrops.

"Son of a... and not one of us is a water witch who can counteract this nonsense," Noel said.

"Where's Faith when you need her?" Abby flipped the windshield wipers on, but the force of the rain was just too much for them.

"I've got this." Noel sat back in the seat, closed her eyes, and imagined a bubble of air in front of the windshield.

"It's working!" Abby called over her shoulder.

"But we're slowing down," Yvette said.

Noel's eyes flew open, and sure enough, the air bubble was slowing the cart down and Wanda's cart was gaining on them.

"Come on!" Yvette urged.

"You've got this, Abby," Noel said. "Keep the pedal to the metal."

"We're going as fast as we can," Abby said, glancing over at Wanda.

Wanda waved as her cart inched past them. Then she threw her head back and laughed. "I can't wait to dig into the Decadent Delights!"

"Nuh-uh," Abby said. Then she pressed a red button on the dash of the cart. For a moment, Noel was sure the booster hadn't worked, and she slumped back into the seat, deflated.

But suddenly, the cart shuddered with energy and darted forward, beating Wanda to the line with only inches to spare.

"Yes, yes, yes, yes!" Abby pulled the cart to a stop, jumped out, and did a crazy dance that involved a lot of butt shaking. "I won! Finally!"

Yvette followed her and the pair of them held hands as they jumped around in a circle.

"She only won because you helped her," Wanda said to Noel, shaking her head in exasperation.

"Maybe," Noel said. "But she's the one that pulled it out in the end. You have to give her credit for that. And we had three people to your two. Just admit it was an impressive win, coming from behind like that."

"Yeah, okay, sure. Impressive. Whatever. I'm still the queen of the golf cart races."

"There's no doubt about that," Noel said, laughing. "Nice job, Hanna. That rain nearly did the trick."

"Thanks. That was fun... even if we didn't win," she said.

"We'll get 'em next time," Wanda said as she climbed into her cart. "Enjoy it, Townsend," Wanda called to Abby as they flew by. "Next time I'll be more than ready for your little tricks."

"I'm gonna have to step up my game," Abby said as she raised the booze thermos and took a victory sip. "Wanda's gonna be plotting for days on how to take me down."

"Oh, Abby. You can worry about that later." Yvette climbed into the driver's seat and with a gleam in her eye, she added, "Right now we need to celebrate. Get in."

"She's right," Noel said, taking the seat next to Yvette. "You just won. Let's enjoy it!"

Abby climbed aboard and said, "Okay, I'm in. Let's celebrate!"

"Whoohoo!" Yvette pressed the pedal to the floor, cranked the wheel, and spun them around in a donut. She let out another whoop and cranked the wheel in the opposite direction. Only instead of the cart turning, it went straight, heading directly for the ditch. "Oh, no! Stop, stop!" Yvette cried, pumping the breaks. "I can't stop. We're going to—*oomph!*"

The cart came to an abrupt halt in a drainage ditch at the bottom of a small slope.

The wheels spun, and mud kicked up, splattering the cart and the three of them in a layer of grime.

Everyone was silent for a few seconds while they processed what had just happened.

"Holy hell," Noel finally said, shakily climbing out of the cart. "What happened?"

"My cart!" Abby cried, emerging from the back seat covered in mud. "Oh my... look at what we've done! Her wheels are submerged."

"The brakes locked-up. I'm so sorry, Abs," Yvette said, tears glittering in her eyes again. "Oh my god, I almost killed us!"

"We're fine," Noel said, grabbing her hand. "Other than an impromptu mud bath and needing a tow out of here, we're perfectly fine. No need to panic."

"Where's my phone?" Abby said, frantically searching her pockets. "I think I lost my phone. Son of a—how are we gonna get out of here? It's a good five miles back to Dad's."

"Relax. I've got mine right here," Noel said and stared at her contacts. "Is Clay available?"

"He should be," Abby said.

Noel pulled up his number and hit Call. Only the voice that answered was not Clay. "Deputy Baker," Noel said. "Is there a reason you're answering my future brother-in-law's phone?"

"Yes," he said, sounding amused. "Clay and I were just getting ready to have a beer, and your name popped up on his screen instead of mine. I might've gotten a little jealous."

"Jealous?" she echoed as she rolled her eyes. "Come on now. Don't be ridiculous."

He chuckled. "There's no controlling the heart, Noel. Now, tell me what my buddy Clay can do for you that I can't?"

"It's not... Um..." Crap. She didn't want to tell him they'd crashed into a ditch. The minute she did that, he'd be on his way to help, and she looked like some dirty sea creature from the black lagoon.

"We need a tow," Abby yelled. "Get in your vehicle and get over here."

"Abby!" Noel said in a hushed whisper. "Shhh."

"What? We need help. If he's with Clay, he's going to find out anyway."

Noel sighed. Her sister had a point.

"What's that? You need a tow? Where are you?" he asked, suddenly alarmed. "Did you hit another car? Are there any injuries? I need details, Noel."

"No one is hurt," she said. "We were out in the golf cart and—"

"You were golf cart racing." His accusation made her grimace, and she felt like she was sixteen all over again and she'd just gotten caught stealing the family car.

"Yes, but we didn't crash while racing," she said defensively. "In fact, we beat the pants off Wanda and Hanna."

"But you did crash? How?"

She sucked in a breath, winced, and said, "Yvette was doing donuts."

CHAPTER 17

"OUR WOMEN ARE STUCK IN A DITCH," Drew said to Clay after he ended the call with Noel.

"Seriously? The golf cart is in a ditch?" Clay asked. "I knew something like this would happen. Abby has lost her mind when it comes to that thing."

"Abby wasn't driving," Drew said, sliding off his stool. He'd stopped into the Keating Hollow Brewery just before closing time on his way back into town from Eureka. They were getting ready to partake of a few beers when he'd seen Noel's name flash on Clay's phone. "It was Yvette."

"Good lord. She's infected her sisters with her crazy golf cart obsession." He grabbed his keys. "Let's go haul them out. Where are they?"

"Down by the river." Drew followed him out of the brewery.

"Of course they are." When they got outside, they glanced between Clay's Jeep and Drew's SUV. All five of them weren't going to fit in the Jeep Wrangler. "I'll follow you," Clay told Drew. "We won't all fit in my vehicle, but we're gonna need it to haul the golf cart home. It's lucky I haven't returned the trailer I borrowed when we picked it up last month."

"Lucky indeed," Drew said with a chuckle. "I'm guessing you should just buy your own, considering this turn of events."

"You have a point," his friend said. Then he narrowed his eyes at Drew. "*Our* women? Does that mean Abby and Noel?"

Drew had hoped Clay had missed that little slip of the tongue. He wasn't sure when he'd started to think of Noel as his, but there it was and there was no turning away from it now. He figured it was better to just own it. Clay wasn't going to let him off the hook anyway. "Yep. Abby and Noel."

"Since when is Noel your woman?" Clay asked as he unlocked his truck and climbed into the driver's seat.

"I guess since earlier today. We uh, had a moment."

"A moment?" Clay laughed. "Is that code for slept together?"

"Get your mind out of the gutter, Garrison." Drew shook his head and retreated to his SUV. "It just means that we might be finally moving out of the friend zone. We have a date tomorrow night."

"Well, it's about damned time," Clay said. They quickly got the trailer attached to the Jeep. Then Clay slammed his door and took off toward the river.

It didn't take them long to find the Townsend sisters. Yvette had used her magic to build a small fire, giving the men an easy beacon to follow.

Drew pulled his SUV to a stop beside the women, who were standing around the makeshift fire pit. "Need a lift?"

Noel's face lit up with a smile, and Drew had to stifle a laugh. She was a complete mess with mud covering half her body and streaked in her hair. But that smile... she radiated with joy. "You have no idea just how glad I am to see you."

He jumped out and opened the door for her. "Get in out of the cold. I'm going to help Clay free that party cart."

Noel started to climb into the front seat but then stopped and turned back to him. "I'm going to get mud everywhere. Do you have a towel or something?"

He shook his head. "Don't worry about it. The leather seats will clean right up."

She groaned. "I'm sorry about this."

"I'm not." He winked at her and turned to Abby and Yvette. "You're welcome to join her."

Abby shook her head. "I'm gonna help Clay with my baby."

"And I'm going to make sure you have light," Yvette added.

"Geez. I can't just sit here while you're all working," Noel said, pushing the car door open.

"You're fine, Noel," Abby said. "I'm not sure there's anything else to do anyway. We'll holler if we need anything."

She hesitated for a moment, but when Drew reached in and turned on the heater, she sat back and said, "Okay. I'll sit this one out."

Damn, she's adorable, Drew thought as he stood there and gazed at her. The fact that mud was smeared down her cheek and her hair was a clumped-together mess just made her all that more real. A vision of stripping her out of her clothes flashed in his mind. What he wouldn't give to be the one who got to wash away all the mud covering her flawless skin.

"Earth to Drew," Clay called. "Wanna get this done tonight, or do we need to reschedule?"

He jerked his attention to his friend. "Huh?"

"Golf cart?" Clay pointed at the vehicle tilted at an angle in the ditch. "Want to hook up the chain so we can haul this thing out of here?"

"Right." He cast one more glance at Noel, smiled, and then got to work.

Twenty minutes later, they'd loaded the cart onto the trailer. Luckily, her "baby" had only suffered a flat tire, and

Clay had promised Abby he'd have her up and running in the next day or two.

"You're the best," she said to her fiancé then nodded to Yvette. "You can kill the fire now. We're ready to go."

"You got it." The firelight winked out, and Yvette started to make her way toward the SUV.

"Vette, we'll give you a ride," Abby said. "Your house is on the way."

The reality was that Yvette lived about equal distance from both Abby and Noel, so it really didn't matter who gave her a lift. But it was pretty clear Abby wasn't going to take no for an answer.

"Besides," Abby added, "I left my private reserve wine sitting on your counter. I have plans for it tomorrow night."

Noel shook her head and muttered something under her breath. Something that sounded a lot like the word *bullshit*.

"Right," Yvette said and climbed into the Jeep. Clay honked as he took off.

Abby leaned her head out the window and called, "Have fun you, two. And when I say fun, I don't mean Scrabble!"

"Your sister is trouble," Drew said after he climbed into the SUV.

"She's had a little too much to drink." Noel fastened her seatbelt. "I bet she pays for that tomorrow."

Drew put the SUV in gear and followed the Jeep lights down the golf cart path. "Doesn't she have a hangover potion or something?"

"Well, sure, but only if she's in decent enough shape to make one. If she's trashed, her magic likely won't be up to snuff." Noel smirked. "It serves her right. Look at what she got us into."

Drew glanced over at her, thoroughly enjoying her company. She was relaxed and letting him see her with all her guards down. He couldn't help but want her even more. "You had a good time, though, right?"

"Sure." She threw her head back and laughed. "The best time. I have a feeling we're going to be telling that story for years."

Drew nodded and silently hoped he'd be by her side to hear it.

All too soon, Drew parked the SUV in front of the inn. Before she could say anything, he jumped out and rushed to open the door for her.

"You didn't have to do that, Drew," she said, giving him a shy, vulnerable smile.

"If it means getting another one of those smiles, then yes, I did." He gently took her hand in his and walked her to the front door.

In the glow of her porch light, she glanced down at herself and grimaced. "Oh, my goddess. I can't believe you're seeing me like this. I look like a swamp creature."

"You look adorable," Drew said and cupped her cheek with one hand. "And, Noel?"

"Yes," she said breathlessly.

"I'm really glad you're okay." He tilted his head down and brushed his lips over hers.

She hesitated for just a moment, but when he gently parted her lips with his tongue, she swayed into him, pliant in his arms. He circled one arm around her waist and pulled her in so that he could feel every inch of her soft body pressed against his.

"So perfect," he whispered and kissed her again, enjoying her faint lime taste.

She giggled and pulled back slightly. "Perfect? I think your standards are a little low, Deputy Baker. It appears I've gotten mud all over you."

Glancing down at his jeans and T-shirt, the plain clothes he'd changed into before heading off to Eureka that afternoon, he shrugged. "I'll happily get dirty with you anytime, Noel."

"Good answer," she said softly. She wrapped her arms around his neck, and this time when her lips met his, they were full of so much passion, Drew was certain he'd never be able to let her go.

CHAPTER 18

WHEN DREW WOKE the next morning, he could still feel Noel's lips on his. It had taken every last ounce of his willpower to not follow her into her home. God knew he wanted to. But it wasn't time. Not yet. He didn't want to get that involved while he was still working the case to find her ex. At least not while she was out of the loop. He'd tell her that night on their date.

After a quick shower, he dressed in plain clothes, grabbed a cup of coffee, and called the office to let Clarissa know he'd be out of town for the day. Then he took off for Yachtsmen's Harbor to follow up on the lead he'd gotten from Sally at Pies, Pies, and More Pies. When he pulled his SUV into the parking lot, he spotted a sign for Pacific Cove Boat Rentals. He nodded. That made sense. That was the other place Xavier had been spotted besides the Moon River Inn.

The sun was out, a rare occurrence for the coast in early December, as Drew made his way to the rental kiosk.

A young brunette was perched on a stool behind the counter. She gave Drew a huge smile and a finger wave, and said, "Well, hello there, handsome."

"Hello…" Drew peered at her nametag, "Whitney. I'm hoping you can help me with something."

"For you? Anything." She leaned forward, putting her weight on her elbows. "Need a boat? Are you headed out to do a little fishing?"

"No. Thank you. I'm Deputy Sheriff Baker, and I'm actually looking for someone." He first pulled out his ID then Xavier's photo. "Can you tell me if you've seen this man?"

Her flirty smile fled the instant her gaze scanned the photo. "Yes. That's the guy who killed Xavier."

Drew's eyebrows shot up. "You mean the man who was found on the beach in Trinidad?"

"Yeah. Him." She jerked back and crossed her arms over her chest. "He went by Victor."

Drew eyed her for just a moment then asked, "What makes you think he killed Xavier?"

"It's always the quiet ones you have to watch out for," she said. "You know, they act all sweet and then BAM! They end up being a stalker or some douche who sleeps with your best friend."

Whoa, Drew thought. *This one has an issue or two.* Ms. Perky had been replaced by Ms. Irrational. "I see. Can you tell me, when was the last time you saw Victor?"

"The day he and Xavier were here to rent the boat. They were supposed to go tuna fishing. The boat went out, but it never came back in."

"Did you see them get on the boat together before they left?"

She shook her head. "Nope. I just do the paperwork. Ralph down at the docks is the one to ask."

"Got it." Drew made a few notes. "You've been very helpful, Whitney. Is there anything else you can remember about that day you think might be important?"

Her eyes narrowed, and her voice turned hard when she said, "Yeah. Xavier deserved what he got. I'm not sorry he's gone."

The fine hairs stood up on the back of Drew's neck. "What did he do to you?"

Her expression turned stony. "Let's just say he got handsy."

"And what about Victor?"

"He wasn't here when it happened, but since they were buddies, I'm sure he wouldn't have given a shit. Men suck."

Drew couldn't argue with her on that one. He'd seen far too much bullshit on the job. Some men did suck. He just nodded. "I'm sorry that happened to you. And again, thank you. You've been a big help."

"You're welcome, Deputy Baker. I hope you catch the other one and put him behind bars for the rest of his life."

"I'll do my best, ma'am." He gave her a kind smile and walked down toward the boats. As it turned out, Ralph couldn't even remember Xavier or Victor, so getting a confirmation that they'd been together that morning was a complete bust. If Xavier had killed his partner, he'd done a damn fine job of making sure there weren't any witnesses. Not that he was trying to prove there was a murder. All he needed to do was find Xavier. The rest was up to someone else in the chain of command.

Drew climbed back into his SUV and sat behind the steering wheel, feeling slightly frustrated. The only leads he had in finding Xavier had been a complete bust. He wasn't even sure where to start looking next.

He pulled out his phone and was just about to give Noel a call to find out how she was doing when a call from Clarissa came in. He answered on the first ring.

"Hey, boss. I have something for you," she said.

Drew grabbed his pen and notebook and said, "Shoot."

"I got the information from the wallet John Doe had on him. The driver's license is completely fake. It's a made-up number, and the address doesn't even exist."

Drew ground his teeth. "Anything else?"

"The credit cards are all prepaid. There haven't been any charges since three days before John Doe was found, which makes perfect sense since they've been sitting in the evidence room. Are you ready for what records we *did* find?"

"Yep. I'm all ears."

"Sunshine Hotel on East Street. Last charge was made a week ago. There's also a few charges to some place called Pies, Pies, and More Pies."

"Anywhere else?" he asked.

"Yeah, some place called Lilies and More. Looks like a flower shop."

"Strange." Drew jotted down the information and said, "Thanks, Clarissa. How are things in town?"

"As boring as ever. Pauly is pricing out jaywalking cams. I keep telling him they aren't in the budget, but he says they'd be cheaper than paying a physical person to keep an eye on things. I'm not sure he understands that he is actively advocating for tech to take over the only thing he's good at."

Drew couldn't help the snort of amusement. "Figures. No one ever said Pauly Putzner was playing with a full deck. If he brings it up again, tell him I vetoed it and that it's time to get to work."

"Will do."

Drew ended the call and pointed his vehicle north on Hwy 101 in the direction of the Sunshine Hotel. The Sunshine, as the locals called it, was a large Victorian in the heart of downtown. It was a bed and breakfast, not unlike Noel's place, only larger. It couldn't have been more different from the Moon River Inn if it tried.

Since there was no parking lot, Drew parallel parked his SUV on the street about a block away and headed toward the hotel. He was about twenty feet from the entrance when a familiar blond-haired man ducked out onto the sidewalk. Drew studied the man for just a second before he called out, "Xavier?"

The man paused and glanced back. Recognition washed over his troubled gaze when he spotted the deputy sheriff. Drew waved as he started forward, intending to act as if they were just old friends bumping into each other, but Xavier wasn't falling for it. Suddenly he bolted, taking off across the street right into oncoming traffic. One car swerved, barely missing him. Another driver slammed on the brakes, and a third laid into his horn, shouting obscenities out the window.

Xavier ignored all of it and ran flat-out toward a black Honda SUV.

"Son of a..." Drew knew there was no way he was going to catch Xavier before he scrambled into the SUV, so he bolted back to his own vehicle. Just as he jammed the key into the ignition, the Honda flew by him, going in the opposite direction. Drew twisted in his seat, trying to get the license plate number, but it was obscured, and he only got the first three characters. 7BN. He started to pull away from the curb but was forced to wait for a wave of traffic to pass him. He tapped his fingers impatiently on the wheel and said, "Come on, come on!"

Finally there was a small opening in traffic, and Drew made an illegal U-turn, taking off after the Honda. He saw the vehicle a block ahead, idling at a red light. But Xavier must've spotted him, because the black Honda shot through the red light, weaved through traffic, and took a right turn, disappearing around the corner. Drew did his best race-car-driver impression and floored it, but when he made the turn, the Honda was gone.

Drew let out a slew of curses, frustrated that he'd lost him and hadn't even been able to get the full license plate number. He had, however, noticed there was a barcode in the back window. It was a rental. And along with a partial hit on the plate, that gave him something to work with.

The deputy sheriff drove around the downtown area, searching for the Honda at least five times before he gave up and headed for Lilies and More. The flower shop, if you could even call it that, was more of a convenience store near a truck stop just north of town. They had buckets of flowers out front, but nothing resembling flower arrangements. Drew went in and inquired about Xavier, but the tattooed man behind the checkout counter just shrugged and went back to reading his *High Times* magazine.

Fresh out of leads, Drew backtracked to the Sunshine Hotel, parked his vehicle down a side street, and headed for a small café across from the hotel. If Xavier came back, Drew would be ready for him. Once he was seated with coffee in front of him, he called Clarissa.

"Hey again, boss. Whatcha need?"

"I need you to track down information on a partial plate. It's a rental car. Get me any information you can." He rattled off the details.

"I'm on it," she said.

CHAPTER 19

THE SHRILL SOUND of the phone ringing made Noel wince. She was nursing a dull headache, thanks to her poor choices the night before. Mixing wine and Moscow Mules was *not* a good idea. Pressing a hand to her forehead, she picked up the receiver and was greeted with a dial tone.

She pulled the phone away from her ear, scowled at it, and placed it back on its cradle. That was the second time she'd picked up the line to find no one on the other end that morning. She was definitely being punished.

The bell on the front door chimed, and Abby strolled in, her head held high and a smile on her face.

"What are you so happy about this morning?" Noel asked.

"I'm still on a high from the race last night." She set a large coffee cup on the counter. "Drink this. It'll make everything right in your world again."

Noel shook her head, already fidgety from too much caffeine. "I've already had two cups of coffee, Abs. I don't think a strong dose of java is my miracle cure this time around."

"Ah, but you haven't had my special blend," she said smugly. "A little magic goes a long way."

Noel looked up from her computer. "You made a coffee hangover potion?"

She spread her arms out wide and dipped into a tiny bow. "You're welcome, dear sister. You should've seen Yvette before I got my concoction down her throat." Abby simulated a shudder. "You'd think death had come for her. But now she's fine and down at her bookstore getting ready for the holiday sale tomorrow."

"Other than too much booze, how's she doing?" Noel took a sip of Abby's coffee and savored the rich smooth flavor. The stuff was better than what they served at the Incantation Café, and that was saying something. "Yum, Abs, this is delicious."

"I have my moments," she said with a smile. "Yvette is doing better than when we found her last night. Though, that's not hard to do. Still, the tears have dried, and she's determined to not let his drama affect her business."

"I suppose Isaac didn't come home last night?" Noel asked.

"Nope. But Yvette said she hadn't expected him too. She says when he's got something in his head, he usually sticks to his guns."

"Sounds familiar," Noel said. "They are two peas in a pod."

"They used to be," Abby agreed. She eyed the cup in Noel's hand. "How's that headache coming?"

"Huh?" Noel glanced down at the now-half-empty cup she was still holding and then grinned. "It's gone. Hells bells, baby sister. You're a genius. I bet you could make a fortune packaging and selling this miracle cure."

"That's what Clay said." She leaned against the check-in counter and crossed one ankle over the other. "But I'm not sure it's ready for prime time. We're thinking about offering it as a takeout item at the Brewery."

Noel chuckled. "I can see the tagline now. *Welcome to Townsend's Keating Hollow Brewery... Where the beer goes down easy and the coffee fixes last night's mistakes.*"

"Cute." She gave Noel a smirk. "Okay. Now dish. What happened last night with Drew?"

"Nothing," Noel said too quickly. "He just dropped me off here."

"Oh?" Abby raised a curious eyebrow. "Is that why I saw you two making out on your front porch after we dropped Yvette off?"

"We weren't making out," Noel insisted. Then she jerked back slightly as she processed what her sister had said. "You drove by the inn after dropping Vette off?"

"Yeah, so?"

"So... you were spying on me! Geez, Abby. There was no reason to backtrack last night, and you know it. You just wanted to see if I invited the deputy inside, didn't you?"

"Fine." Abby threw her hands up in mock exasperation. "I admit it. But it's not my fault there was massive PDA going on. It's not like you were trying to hide anything from anyone. You were right under the porch light."

Noel giggled like a school girl, thoroughly enjoying the exchange with her sister. Yes, she was slightly annoyed that Abby had intentionally spied on her and Drew, but she'd missed this sisterly bonding, the good-natured ribbing, and more importantly, the obvious desire to see that each of them was happy. Knowing that someone was one thousand percent in your corner was priceless. "I might not have really cared who saw us in that moment."

"Obviously."

The inn's phone rang again. Noel snagged it. "Keating Hollow Inn."

Silence.

"Hello?"

Nothing.

"Anyone there?"

Click.

Noel scowled at the phone and once again placed it back on its base. "That is the third time today that someone has called and hung up."

"Really? That's rude," Abby said, smoothing her ponytail.

"It's creepy. It makes me feel like I'm being stalked or something."

"Any heavy breathing?" Abby grabbed one of the witch cookies Drew had left on the counter the day before.

Noel shook her head. "No. The first two times they hung up before I could even answer. And this one... they seemed to be trying to decide if they wanted to say something but then didn't."

She shrugged. "Maybe someone has social anxiety and they are working their way up to asking for a room."

"Maybe. But if that's the case, they can book online."

"You got me there." Abby waved the cookie. "This is delicious. You should keep these out all the time."

Noel felt butterflies in her stomach when she said, "Drew brought those."

Abby clutched her heart. "My goodness. Could he be any more adorable?"

No. He really couldn't.

"HEY SWEETHEART," Noel said as Daisy climbed into the car. "How was your day?"

She didn't look at her mother as she said, "It was okay."

Noel frowned. Something was off with her daughter. It was

Friday, school had just gotten out, and Daisy had plans with Olive for a sleepover that night. Noel had expected her kid to be bouncing off the walls. "Something happen?"

"No." She hugged her backpack and stared down at her lap.

Noel didn't press the issue while she carefully navigated the school pickup line, but the moment they got home, she told Daisy to let Buffy out of her kennel and to take her out. Her daughter did as she was told and perked up slightly when she buried her face in Buffy's brindled fur, but her normally exuberant kid was missing in action.

"Want some hot cocoa? How about a snack?" Noel asked, already pulling the cocoa mix out of the cabinet.

"No thanks, Mommy. I'm just going to go play with Buffy," Daisy said, leaving her mother standing in the kitchen with her mouth gaping open.

"Was that my kid?" Noel asked no one. She shoved the cocoa back into the cabinet and made her way to the living room.

Daisy was sprawled on the floor with her head propped on a throw pillow, petting Buffy, who was lying on her chest.

Noel sat down next to her daughter and gave Buffy a scratch behind the ear. "What's up, baby? Are you feeling okay?"

"Yeah," she said, but she didn't look at her mother.

"Tired after your night with Auntie Faith? Did Xena and Buffy keep you up?"

She shook her head. "They both slept with me. Auntie Faith said it was the first time Xena had slept through the night since she got her." Daisy glanced at her mother and gave her a small smile. "I think she loves me best."

Noel chuckled. "You're probably right." Even with the small spark of life, this version of Daisy was so subdued, Noel worried her daughter was keeping something from her. She'd been fine when Noel had picked her up from her dad's house and dropped her off at school. Or maybe she was just completely worn out. Daisy didn't spend too many nights away from Noel and almost never on a school night. Maybe that had been a mistake. Whatever it was, Noel didn't feel comfortable sending her to Abby's while she spent the evening with Drew. Not when Daisy was so obviously not acting like herself.

"Listen, Daisy," Noel said. "What do you say about the two of us having a special Mommy daughter night? We can stay in, make lasagna, and bake holiday cupcakes. Maybe watch Frozen?"

She popped up, her eyes big and full of alarm. "But, Mom. I'm going to Olive's, remember? It's puppy sleepover night."

"I know, but if you're too tired, you can do it another night," Noel said reasonably.

"I'm not tired." She wrapped her hands around Buffy and held her close. "Besides, Buffy is excited to see Endora."

Noel stifled a chuckle. Endora was Olive's golden retriever puppy, and Noel was certain it was Daisy who was excited to see her. "Okay. It's fine. You can go to Aunt Abby's and have your puppy sleepover. I just didn't want you to overdo it."

"I'm fine," she reiterated and then got up and carried Buffy to her room.

"Okay then." Noel let her daughter be and disappeared into the kitchen to make cupcakes anyway. Just because Daisy wasn't interested in a sugar high, it didn't mean Noel wasn't.

An hour later, Daisy appeared in the kitchen, her overnight bag in one hand and her empty backpack in the other. Without a word, she took it upon herself to pack dog food, puppy treats, a couple of Buffy's balls, and Buffy's blanket from her crate. When she was done, she slipped the backpack on and told her mother, "We're ready now."

Noel couldn't speak. She was too choked up. Goodness,

how cute was that? Her child was the most adorable human on the planet. Noel crouched down and ruffled her daughter's curly dark locks. "You're the best doggie mama. You know that?"

Daisy beamed.

"Come here." Noel opened her arms wide, and her daughter fell into her, holding on tight.

"I love you, Mama," Daisy said, her voice muffled against Noel's shoulder.

"I love you, too, baby."

They held each other for a long moment, and then Noel finally pulled back and took a good look at Daisy. Her eyes were bright, and her cheeks were rosy. She didn't look tired or upset. Still, even though Noel couldn't put her finger on it, she knew something wasn't quite right with her daughter.

Then Daisy grinned at her and pointed to her fluff ball of a dog. "Buffy's ready to go."

The puppy was sitting at Noel's feet, her tongue out and her tail thumping. As soon as Noel looked down at her, Buffy ran to the door and barked.

Noel laughed. "Come on, then. I'm sure Endora can't wait for her playmate to get there."

Ten minutes later, Noel, Daisy, and Buffy were welcomed into the Garrison household. The second they stepped inside, Olive and Daisy ran off squealing with both their puppies chasing after them. Whatever had been bothering Daisy seemed to have vanished as soon as she saw Olive. Noel let out a sigh of relief. If being around her soon-to-be cousin was what she needed, then Noel was on board.

"You're going to have an exciting night," Noel said to Abby. "Two screaming kids and their dogs. You sure you don't need help?"

"Don't even try it, Noel Townsend. You have a date tonight.

Olive already ratted you out. It seems someone was trying to entice her child to stay home so she didn't have to go out on her date." Abby tsked. "Not on my watch, missy. You've been waiting for this date for how long? Years, right?"

"Abby—" Noel said with a sigh.

"Don't even start, big sis," she said, shaking her head. Then she started in on a lecture about how Noel couldn't close herself off forever, and that she had to know that adult relationships were important, and that she deserved to be loved.

Noel let her go on and on, because it seemed Abby might have been talking from a place of experience. When she finally paused, Noel put a hand on her arm and said, "Abs, I appreciate the ah... pep talk, but I wasn't trying to get out of my date with Drew. I was just worried about Daisy. She was pretty despondent when I picked her up from school. And when we got home, she seemed tired or stressed. I don't know what's going on, but when I suggested we stay home, she closed the door on that pretty hard. And obviously, she's excited to be here. So... Are you going to help me pick what I'm going to wear, or are you just going to keep lecturing me?"

"Oh," Abby said, her expression one of surprise. Then she cleared her throat. "In that case, we need to go shopping."

"I don't think we have time," Noel said.

"Sure we do." Abby took off down the hall and waved for her sister to join her.

Noel followed her into the master bedroom. The space was still pretty masculine, with dark contemporary furniture, a beige bedspread, and tan carpet. If it hadn't been for the candles on the dresser and nightstands and the bright paintings depicting sun streaming through the redwood forest, the room would've been pure bachelor.

"What are we doing in here?" Noel asked her sister.

Abby grinned and pulled the closet doors open. "We're going to give you a makeover."

Noel put her hand out and started to back up. "I don't—"

"Oh no you don't. You are not wearing jeans and a sweater on your official first date."

Noel rolled her eyes. "He's already seen me covered in mud. I don't think he's going to be put off by my jeans. You saw us on my front porch, remember?"

"True." Abby tilted her head to the side and studied her sister. "Still, let's give him something to drool over, shall we?"

Noel listened to her sister chatter on about how excited she was for her, and how great it would be if Noel and Drew ended up together.

"We could double date," Abby said, her expression joyous. "How fun would that be? Clay and Drew are best friends after all. We wouldn't have any of that awkwardness between our significant others when trying to force a foursome. It would be just like old times."

"Not quite like old times, Abby," Noel said quietly. "You'd need Charlotte here for that."

Abby dropped one of the dresses she'd just pulled out of her closet and spun around, a horrified look on her face. "Oh, Noel. No. That isn't what I meant at all."

Noel sat on the edge of the bed and was suddenly exhausted. She reached for her purse and pulled out a couple of the supplements Gerry had given her and popped them in her mouth. When she finally glanced up at her sister, Abby had tears in her eyes. "I'm sorry I upset you," Noel said, feeling awful for saying anything at all. "I just... I always worry Drew thinks I'm a replacement for Charlotte. And I sure as heck don't want to be her replacement in your eyes."

"Is that really what you think?" Abby moved to sit next to her sister.

Noel shrugged. "She was your best friend."

"*You* were my other best friend, Noel," Abby choked out. "I never once wanted you to replace her. I just wanted *you* back. When I left, I lost you. You wouldn't talk to me and you never forgave me for leaving. But I'm back and I'm trying. I thought maybe... hell it doesn't matter what I thought. I love you, Noel. I miss my sister and the friendship we had. I'm sorry I left, but I didn't leave you. I was trying to outrun the pain." She shrugged one shoulder. "Turns out that doesn't work so much. The only way to move on is to confront the past I guess. Can we do that? Do you think you can finally forgive me?"

Pain clutched at Noel's heart as she remembered how devastated she'd been when Abby had left town. "I talked to you. You're the one who stopped answering your phone."

"Because you kept demanding I come back here. I just needed time, Noel," Abby said, sounding tired. "When I tried to connect later, you weren't interested."

Of course Noel had been interested. She'd just been too hurt. Those damned tears were back, silently rolling down her cheeks. "I'm sorry, Abby. I just missed you. Everything here was falling apart. And I... well, when you left, it brought up a bunch of crap from when Mom abandoned us. I was a mess for a while. I guess neither of us handled it well."

Abby clutched her sister's hand. "The last thing I want you to think is that I didn't miss you. I did. All the time. And I certainly didn't leave *you*. Not like what Mom did to us. You have to know that. You were the one I wanted to talk to when my life was out of control. Maybe I wouldn't have wasted so much time on that loser ex of mine if I'd had you around to not sugar coat anything. I love Faith, but she's too nice."

Noel laughed. Faith had spent some time with Abby and her New Orleans boyfriend, and even though Faith hadn't cared for him, she'd been reluctant to say anything to Abby about it. "You're probably right about that." Noel turned to Abby. "Let's make a pact."

"What kind of pact?" Abby asked.

"That if either of us is being a jackass, the other one will kick our butt. No dating douches, and no more silence. We talk it out, even if it kills us."

"Done." Abby spit in her hand and held it out.

"Gross." Noel wrinkled her nose. "What is wrong with you?"

"Would you prefer a blood pact?" Abby asked.

Grimacing, Noel shook her head. Then she spit in her palm and shook Abby's hand. "It's a pact."

When they pulled their hands away, each of them quickly wiped their palms on the other's jeans. Abby threw her head back and laughed. When she sobered she said, "Damn, I really missed you."

"Me too, Abs. Me too." Noel stood and walked over to Abby's closet. "Now, let's find me something to wear that isn't covered in saliva."

CHAPTER 20

AFTER SPENDING MORE than five hours camped out in the café, waiting for Xavier to return to the Sunshine Hotel, Drew finally threw in the towel and headed back to Keating Hollow. There was no guarantee that Xavier would return, especially now that he knew he'd been spotted. If he wanted to stay in the wind, chances were slim-to-none that he'd reemerge in the vicinity any time soon. Drew did, however, call Sheriff Barnes and let him know when and where Xavier had been spotted. The sheriff said he'd put eyes on the location and let him know if anything turned up.

In the meantime, Drew had a date to get to. And he'd be damned if he was going to be late. Not after last night. Not after he'd had to physically tear himself away from the woman who was driving him slightly insane.

The soles of his shoes clicked on the cobbled sidewalk as Drew made his way to the Keating Hollow Inn. After he'd gotten home, he'd quickly showered and shaved and then dressed in slacks and a sport coat. He couldn't help but wonder if he was overdressed. Keating Hollow was, for the most part, a casual town. And so was Noel for that matter. She was always stylish, but she was stylish in jeans and boots instead of dresses and high heels.

This was still a first date though, and he was determined to sweep her off her feet. Drew stepped into the lobby of the Keating Hollow Inn and stopped dead in his tracks when he saw the gorgeous creature behind the counter.

Noel had her blond hair swept up in some sort of fancy bun, and she was wearing a deep violet dress that hugged her curves in all the right places.

"Hello, gorgeous."

She glanced up, seemingly startled to find him there, then a slow smile spread across her face. "Well, hello there, handsome. Who knew the town deputy cleaned up so nicely?"

Drew strode over to her, took her by the hand, and pulled her out from behind the desk, revealing her lace-up boots. "Perfect," he said. "Absolutely stunning."

"Now you're just overselling. Stop before you embarrass yourself," she teased.

"Never. Ready?"

"Yep. Let me just get my coat." She pulled a wool jacket out of the closet behind her, then called out, "Alec! I'm on my way out. See you in the morning."

A door opened on the other side of the lobby, and her employee poked his head out. "'Night, Ms. Townsend," he said. "Enjoy your evening."

"You too." She waved at him then followed Drew outside.

"Do you mind walking?" he asked her as he slipped his arm around her waist, enjoying that faint citrus scent that seemed to cling to her everywhere she went.

"Not at all." Noel leaned into him. "I love seeing our town all lit up for the holidays. It just seems so... joyful."

Joyful. That was exactly how he felt, only he wasn't sure it was the lights that were the cause. They made small talk while they made their way to the restaurant. Drew had taken care of getting them a reservation, and their table was waiting for them when they got there.

"Wine?" Drew asked her.

She hesitated for a moment before letting out a nervous laugh. "I'm not sure wine is a good idea after last night."

"Rough morning?" he asked, completely amused.

"It was until Abby showed up with her magical hangover potion. I swear, she has more talent in her pinky toe than the rest of this town combined."

"What are you saying, Noel? That no one else has magical skills that can impress you?"

"Not exactly," she said with a chuckle. "I'm just saying now that Abby has hit her stride, she's a badass. So if you want to impress me with your magic, you're probably going to have to work for it."

"Challenge accepted," he said.

Dinner was a delicious array of lobster bisque, tuna tartare, and the most flavorful steak Drew had ever had the pleasure of tasting, and still, the food was nothing next to the pleasure he derived from spending the evening with Noel. By the time he paid the bill—he just couldn't let Noel pick up the tab on their first date, no matter how much she protested—Drew was wondering what he'd been waiting for. Why had he decided she was off limits?

Because her family reminded him of someone else he'd loved. Only now, Charlotte's memory wasn't as painful as it had been in the past. When he thought of her, he no longer immediately conjured up the morning she'd been found in Abby's shed, no longer saw her unseeing eyes. Now he remembered she'd been full of life and determined to live it to the fullest.

He frowned, wondering when that shift had happened.

"What's wrong, Drew?" Noel asked.

"Huh?"

"I lost you there for a second. You just zoned-out like you went to another dimension."

"I'm here," he said. "I was reflecting on the wonderful meal we just shared."

Her expression was skeptical when she narrowed her eyes and said, "Somehow I don't think that was the whole truth, but it was a wonderful meal, so I'll let it go."

Chuckling, he stood and held out his hand to her. "Come take an after dinner walk with me. I want to show you something."

That piqued her interest. "Oh, a surprise?"

"Something like that."

Noel linked her arm with his, and Drew thought it was the most natural thing in the world having this woman by his side. And he knew then, in that very moment, that he wasn't going to be able to let her go.

The cold air washed over him, but he barely felt it as he guided the gorgeous woman on his arm down Main Street. They walked arm-in-arm through their town, the one they'd grown up in and the one he was certain both of them would stay in as they lived out the rest of their days. They both had invested every inch of themselves in the enchanted town, her with her inn and him with his commitment to keeping the place safe and as free of crime as possible. He couldn't imagine two people who were more right for each other.

"So, about those protection spells I was talking about," Noel said, pulling him out of his thoughts.

"Protection spells?" he asked, wondering if he'd missed part of the conversation.

"The ones for the New Year's Day festival. We never did talk about them."

He recalled the day Noel had intervened when Shannon had trapped him outside A Spoonful of Magic and she'd said the town was booked up for the New Year's celebration. "Right. And we discussed reinforcing the security spells around town. What about them?"

"You need help, right? Pauly Putzner seems like he can barely boil water, much less cast a spell. Just let me know when you want to get on that and I'm happy to help."

"How about just after Christmas before the town fills up for the New Year's Festival?"

"Perfect." She grinned.

"Now, be nice to Pauly, Noel," Drew teased, completely amused and pleased to be working with her if only for one day. "Can you imagine being a water witch and not even knowing how to swim? That's got to sting."

Noel snorted her amusement. "You know, I'd feel bad for him if he wasn't such a putz. Did you know he tried to give Miss Maple a ticket today for double parking in front of the station?"

Drew frowned. "No. Why was she double parked?"

"She was dropping off holiday gift baskets at the station. One for you, Clarissa, and Pauly. Did you not get yours?"

"Geez, he really is a putz." Drew felt a pang of guilt for not filling her in on his assignment to find Xavier. And now that he'd spotted him, it was only fair that she knew he was nearby, wasn't it? "And, no, not yet. I've been in the field all day."

"Oh, mysterious sheriff stuff," she said with a gleam in her eye. "Were you out running down bad guys?"

"Maybe." He took her hand in his and tugged her down the walking path that led to the river. "Listen, Noel, there's something I have to tell you."

Her amused expression vanished. "Uh-oh. This sounds serious."

"It is." He nodded to a bench near the river's edge. "Can we sit for a few minutes?"

"Sure." She took a seat and turned to him, holding her hands in her lap. "I have to admit, Drew, you're kinda scaring me a little. What is it that's so important?"

He sucked in a short breath and took her hands in his. "A couple of days ago, the county sheriff came to see me. He told me they're short-staffed and didn't have the manpower to try to track down Xavier."

She blinked. "So no one is looking for him in connection to the murder of that other man? Not even to see if he knew him or knew who'd have a beef with him?"

"No." Drew shook his head. "Someone *is* looking for him. That's what the sheriff wanted to talk to me about. He said he wanted someone outside of his department to look into the matter. He didn't tell me why exactly, but I have my suspicions. Anyway, for the foreseeable future, I'm the guy in charge of finding your ex."

Noel pulled her hands from his and sat back into the bench.

Drew frowned, his fingers aching to reach out and take hers again, but he knew this was not the time.

"What are your suspicions?" Her expression was hard and closed-off, completely different from the woman he'd gotten closer to over the last week.

"I'm going to tell you, but I need a promise from you first," he said.

"And what's that, Drew? That I'll still date you even though you've known about this for a couple of days and are just now telling me?"

Whoa. He hadn't expected quite *that* much backlash. He had just started investigating. Except... they *had* made out on her porch the night before and he hadn't mentioned it. Still, he was only doing his job.

"If I hadn't asked what you did all day, would you have told me at all?" she added.

"Noel," he said, taken aback by the accusation in her tone. "Of course I was going to tell you. I just wanted to wait until I had something to tell. Why are you so upset?"

She sucked in a deep breath and blew it out slowly. Then she met his gaze with a cool one of her own. "If you haven't noticed, Deputy Baker, I have a few trust issues. After your husband up and leaves without even a note and your best friend stops talking to you through no fault of your own, one starts to get jaded."

Drew didn't say anything for a moment while he processed what she'd said. "You mean Abby? When she left and ended up in New Orleans?"

Tears filled her big blue eyes as she glared at him. "No. Not Abby. She didn't stop talking to me, she just stopped listening. Though her leaving certainly didn't help."

"Then…" he trailed off as he remembered a long-ago conversation at the end of the summer they'd spent practically joined at the hip. His words came back to him. *I don't think we can do this, Noel. It's better if we just remain friends.*

Only they hadn't remained friends. Not real ones, anyway. They saw each other around town and were polite. They made small talk about the weather, the brewery, how their families were doing, but not anything close to the vest. Nothing *real*. Not like how they'd been with each other during that summer when they'd both been counselors at Camp-us Pocus, the sleepaway camp for preteen witches. At Camp-us Pocus, they'd talked about everything, including Charlotte and the pain they'd each suffered with her loss; Drew because she'd been his first love, and Noel because she'd lost both a friend and her sister, who'd been unable to deal with her guilt and pain.

And when they weren't dealing with the fallout of Charlotte's death, they'd been there for each other in other ways, like helping to work out how they were going to pursue their dreams. She'd even shared her plan to open the inn with him way back then. They'd been so close that wherever one was, the other one was sure to follow. But then Drew had made the mistake of kissing her and promptly freaked out because he was in no way ready for another relationship, especially not a relationship with Abby Townsend's sister. He'd spent a lot of time blaming Abby for something that ultimately hadn't even been remotely her fault. But he'd been in too much pain to see it.

For years after that, he'd had trouble being around the Townsend household just because the memories were too hard, not because he resented them or blamed them. It was only since Abby had come back to town and Drew had been forced to interact with her that he realized all that crap was just in his head. He was done grieving Charlotte. He'd always love her and what they had, but he was done.

"I'm sorry, Noel. You didn't deserve the way I treated you," Drew said, staring into her haunted eyes. "My only excuse is that I was young and in a lot of pain. I think I felt like I was betraying Charlotte. Instead of trying to explain what was going on, I just bolted. I know I hurt you, and for that I sincerely apologize."

"Thank you," she said in a small voice as she stared at the rushing river.

"One more thing."

She glanced back at him, her eyes still bright with unshed tears. "What?"

"You should know that I'm not that guy anymore. My days

of running are long gone." He pressed a palm to her cheek. "I know what's important in my life, and who. Don't think for a minute I'm going to forget."

She opened her mouth, closed it, then visibly swallowed as her eyes cleared. "Who's important to you, Drew?"

"You are, Noel. You and Daisy. And that is why I'm determined to find your ex."

Her eyebrows furrowed together as she frowned. "You're determined to find him for… me and Daisy? Why? Are you trying to get out of dating me, because if that's what this is—"

"Noel," he said softly with a small amused smile. "I am most definitely *not* trying to get out of dating you. In fact, I'm actively pleading my case so you don't dump me."

Her frown disappeared and was replaced by something that resembled confusion. "Okay, so why are you trying to find Xavier?"

"So that you and Daisy can have closure. I know that his leaving tore you up. And it's not just the fact that he left, but the *way* he did it. You deserve answers, but more importantly, so does Daisy. Is she still having nightmares?"

Noel frowned. She couldn't remember discussing Daisy's anxiety with him. "How did you know about those?"

"I accidentally overheard Abby and Clay talking about it when she was making up her potions. I wasn't trying to eavesdrop, it just sorta happened. I'm sorry if that bothers you."

"It's fine, Drew," she said and patted his knee.

His gaze landed on her hand. She was touching him again, and her tone had softened. Both were good signs. But he still had things to say.

"Now about Xavier—" he started.

"Have you found the jackass yet?" Noel asked.

"I came close today."

Her mouth fell open. "You... found him?"

"In Eureka. He was staying at the Sunshine Hotel. I was checking on a lead, getting ready to head inside when suddenly, there he was, walking out of the hotel."

"Holy balls," she whispered. "What did you do?"

"Unfortunately, he spotted me. I was in plain clothes, and he obviously recognized me because he bolted. He jumped in his SUV and flew like a bat out of hell down Hwy 101. I tried to follow, but I had to get back to my vehicle. By the time I made a U-turn, he was gone. I waited all day to see if he'd show back up, but no such luck. Then I came back here and took my favorite girl to dinner."

She smirked. "Don't try to charm me out of my... whatever crazy mood I just slipped into."

"It's working, though."

Her smirk turned to a smile as she gazed at him.

"There it is, that smile I've come to love so much." He ran his thumb over her jawline and leaned in, brushing a kiss across her cheek. When he pulled back, he gestured to the river.

Noel let out a tiny gasp of surprise. "Are you... you're making that happen, aren't you?"

He shrugged one shoulder while concentrating on the elaborate water display he'd conjured with just his mind. Streams of water shot straight up in the air, forming a stem, while droplets of water danced around, forming daisy flower petals.

"Drew," she whispered, her voice barely audible. "That might be the sweetest thing anyone has ever done for me."

He slipped his hand in hers and said, "I just hope I have an opportunity to top myself."

She glanced down at their entwined hands. "You're being very sweet. But there are a few things I need to say, too."

"Okay. Shoot."

"I've already told you I have trust issues," she said.

"Yes, you did." He met her gaze, staring intently. "I'm a patient man."

"It would appear, Andrew Baker, that you indeed are. But if we're going to move forward, there's something I need to make clear."

"Lay it on me, Noel," he said, ready to accept whatever it was she had to say.

"I just don't think I can do this if I'll always be playing second fiddle to Charlotte."

Drew jerked back, momentarily stunned by her words.

"Drew, I—"

"Do I make you feel like you're my second choice?" he asked, a little bit hurt and a lot confused. He hadn't spoken about Charlotte in a long time.

She was quiet for a couple beats and finally said, "No. Not now. But I've been here once before."

"Noel... that was a long time ago."

She nodded. "You're right. It was. And I'm probably not being fair, but I can't help being cautious." She grimaced and glanced away. "I'm sorry. This isn't how I wanted the night to go."

Drew brought their hands to his lips and kissed her fingers. "I'm not."

"Not what?"

"Sorry. This night has gone exactly as I'd hoped." He gave her a gentle smile. "I have no problem reassuring you that you, Noel, don't come second to anyone. Not now. Not ever. All those years ago when we were friends, I just needed to heal. I won't deny I have a few scars, but who doesn't?"

She tightened her fingers around his but didn't respond.

"If you're ready to move forward with this thing, if you think you can trust me, then I'm all-in."

"All-in?" she asked.

He nodded. "All-in. You. Me. Daisy. Buffy. And the rest of your giant family."

She pressed her hand to his cheek, her eyes bright with something that looked a lot like love, something he hadn't seen reflected back at him in a very long time. Then she said, "I'm in, too."

He let out a breath he hadn't known he'd been holding and covered her mouth with his, pouring his entire heart into making sure she knew he was hers. He'd meant it when he'd said he was all-in, and there wasn't any going back now.

"Whoa," she said when they finally broke apart. "That was some kiss."

"There's more where that came from," he said, moving in again.

She just laughed as she stood and pulled him up off the bench. "Take me home, Drew."

Disappointment crashed through him. He wasn't ready for the date to end, not by a longshot.

Her smiled widened as she shook her head. "Don't look at me like I just stole your puppy. I want to take *you* home with me."

"Oh, I see." Then he grinned down at her and said, "I can't wait to see what's under that dress."

"I just bet you can't." She winked at him, and taking a few steps backward, she started to lead the way home.

CHAPTER 21

NOEL MADE her way up the path to Abby's house with two cups of coffee and a bag of pastries in hand. She hadn't gotten much sleep the night before, but despite that fact, she still had a pep in her step. There was no way to know if her newfound energy was a direct result from her night with Drew or the supplements she was taking, but if she had to bet on it, she'd say she was energized because of Drew. Finally taking that next step with him and waking up in his arms had left her not only content but oddly settled. As if everything about them was just right. She'd loved Xavier when they'd been together, before he'd imploded their lives, but even with him she hadn't ever felt that peaceful.

Before Noel reached the stoop, Abby flung the door open and said, "Thank you, sweet goddess of heaven. We ran out of coffee, and I'm dying for my caffeine."

Noel laughed and handed her sister one of the cups. "I have coffee cake, too."

"You're an angel. Save a piece for Yvette. She's on her way over. Now get in here out of the cold." Abby tugged her inside the warm house. Olive and Daisy were playing cards quietly in the middle of the living room with Buffy and Endora curled up next to them.

"Um, what did you do, give them a calming potion?" Noel asked and waved at her daughter. "Hi sweetie. Did you have a good time?"

Daisy nodded and went back to her cards, seemingly uninterested in the fact that her mother had arrived.

"Apparently so," Noel said and followed Abby to the bright kitchen in the back of the house.

"Okay, so first off, I'm dying to hear how the date went."

A huge grin spread across Noel's face as she said, "It went well."

"How well?" Abby asked, eyeing her with suspicion. "Like, if I would've driven by your inn last night, I'd have seen you making out on your front porch well? Or that I'd have found Drew's car parked out front this morning well?"

Noel's face flushed, and her insides turned to mush as she remembered how Drew had woken her this morning with hot passionate kisses. "Um, his car was parked out front."

"Yes! It's about time you had a little fun," Abby said, a wicked gleam in her bright blue eyes. But soon enough her smile faded, and she added, "I'm really happy for you, Noel, and I don't want to spoil your good mood, but I need to fill you in on a few things."

Noel sat at Abby's counter and pulled out the coffee cake, trying not to give in to the sudden fear that gripped her. "Is it Dad?"

Abby shook her head. "No. His ankle is still sore, but otherwise, he's fine."

Noel let out a sigh of relief. Everything else was manageable. "Okay. I'm ready."

"Last night was a little rough," Abby said, sitting next to her sister. "I gave Daisy her calming potion like always, but just after midnight, she woke up crying for her dad."

Noel sighed, frustrated. "Yeah. That happens sometimes. Not as often as it used to, but it happens. Did she calm down?"

"Yes, but she was crying for him to not leave her *again*. She said it over and over again as if he'd come back. I think she might've overheard you or someone else talking about him being nearby, because this just felt… different. More intense."

Since Abby had moved in with Clay, Daisy and Olive had become close, and Daisy had slept over with them two or three times in the last month. This wasn't Abby's first go-round with the nightmares. Noel bit down on her lower lip. "It's possible, but I'm very careful to not talk about him when she's around. Do you think she might've overheard you and Clay?"

"I hope not," Abby said with a frown. "We're pretty careful as well. We don't even talk about him when Olive is around."

Noel nodded. "I suppose if he really is hanging out in Eureka, chances are high we can't keep his presence a secret anyway. I just hope he stays the heck away. She doesn't need that kind of heartbreak again."

"Neither do you," Abby said, giving her a sympathetic smile.

Noel waved a hand. "He can't hurt me. I'm over him. I'm just worried about Daisy. How did you calm her down?"

"I gave her some more potion. She calmed down, but she couldn't get back to sleep and kept asking for Buffy. I finally caved and let them share a bed. She was asleep within five minutes."

Noel smiled. "Those two… I should've remembered to tell you that Buffy sleeps in Daisy's bed now. That might have saved you waking up to a nightmare. She hasn't had one at our place since the first night we brought Buffy home. She's turned into Daisy's comfort animal. And she's such a good puppy. For all my angst at Dad for forcing her on us, I should really give him a huge thank-you gift."

"Like a puppy?" Abby laughed.

"That would serve him right."

"Abby? Noel?" Yvette strode into the kitchen clutching a large Manilla envelope. Her eyes were dry, but they were red and puffy as if she'd just had a good cry.

"Hey," Noel said, jumping up to wrap an arm around her big sister. "What's going on?"

She sucked in a deep breath. "I just need some sister time."

"You got it," Abby said. "Can I get you anything? Tea? Wine? A shovel?"

Yvette let out a startled laugh and plopped down on one of the barstools. "The shovel and anything with sugar in it."

"Coming right up." Noel slid a piece of the coffee cake in front of her. "Abby will have to handle the shovel. Now what's going on?"

She tossed the envelope on the counter. "Isaac filed for divorce. He kindly hand-delivered these to me this morning." Her lips twisted into a grimace. "He said he wanted to explain and that he never intended to hurt me. It's all because of that stupid gym membership I got him."

Noel and Abby shared a knowing glance. They both knew where this was heading.

"Who is it?" Abby asked. "That woman who runs the yoga classes? Or the one who tortures people in spin class? I know, it's the receptionist. She's always touching everyone a little too much."

"I doubt it's her," Noel said to Abby. "She has a girlfriend."

"Oh." Abby frowned. "Probably not likely then."

"It's his accountant," Yvette said, sounding completely defeated. "They met in a spin class."

"Wait," Noel said, confused. "I thought his accountant was Jake Jackson."

"That's right," Yvette said, her eyes full of sadness.

"Isaac is leaving you for Jake?" Abby blurted. "You've got to be kidding me."

"Isaac says he didn't mean for it to happen." Yvette tore off a piece of the coffee cake but didn't eat it. "What does that even mean... he didn't mean for this to happen? Did he just black out one night and end up in bed with another man? I just... how could he do this to me?"

Noel soothed Yvette's untamed dark hair and said, "I'm so sorry, Vette. I'm sure he just means he didn't want to hurt you. It doesn't make it okay that he cheated on you or fell in love with someone else, though."

She sat on the stool staring straight ahead. "How could I have not known?"

"Known what, sweetie?" Noel asked. "That he was interested in men or that he was having an affair?"

She turned and stared Noel in the eyes. "Both."

"Because he hid it from you," Abby said. "This isn't your fault. You did nothing wrong, okay? Do you understand, Yvette? Maybe Isaac really did, and even still does, love you. I know you don't want to hear this right now, but if his interest is in men, then he's doing you a favor. A huge one. You deserve someone who is all-in, crazy in love and lust with you and only you."

"But I gave him eleven years. Eleven years!" she cried. "I don't deserve this. I was a great wife. I hope Jake stomps all over his heart."

"Oh, honey," Abby said and wrapped her arms around her. Noel did the same, and the pair of them held on to Yvette, trying their best to keep her from breaking apart.

CHAPTER 22

DREW SAT at his desk going over some notes. He'd spent the last three days trying to track down Xavier. They'd gotten a hit off the partial license plate in the system and now had an alert out that the person who'd rented the Honda was a person of interest in an ongoing case. They'd gotten four tips in the last few days, and Drew had spent most of his time following up over in Eureka.

Despite checking out a movie theater, a fish shack, a laundromat, and a drug store, so far Drew had turned up nothing. According to their respective staffs, Xavier hadn't been back to either the Moon River Inn, the Sunshine Hotel, nor Pies, Pies, and More Pies. Now Drew was staring at a map, trying to pinpoint a central location where Xavier might be holed-up. So far he wasn't having any luck.

He got up and started to pace. It didn't help that he couldn't get Noel out of his mind. The night they'd spent together had rocked him to his core. He'd told her he was all-in and had meant it, but after they'd spent the night together, he knew he was a goner. She couldn't get rid of him if she tried. He'd never wanted a woman the way he wanted her. The past few nights, he'd spent an hour or two with her in her porch swing. And both nights, he'd loathed to leave. But she had Daisy, and they'd just started officially dating. Neither thought subjecting her to sleepovers was appropriate.

He glanced at the clock. It was just before noon, and he had a lunch date to get to. He was meeting Noel at the brewery during her break. But just as he was getting ready to step outside, his phone buzzed. It was the Eureka office. "Baker."

"Deputy, we've got a sighting of that vehicle again. It's parked down at the Pacific Cove Boat Rentals. So far no one matching Anderson's description had been spotted."

"Thanks. I'm on my way." He informed Clarissa he was on his way out and then called Noel. When she didn't answer, he quickly sent her a text and jumped into his SUV.

Twenty-five minutes later, Drew pulled into the Pacific Cove Marina parking lot and spotted the Honda almost instantly. It was sitting right next the exit. And damn, if he didn't get lucky. Xavier was in the driver's seat, and he was staring right at Drew. Drew stared back. When Xavier didn't take off, Drew inched his SUV right up alongside the Honda and pressed the button to lower his window.

"Xavier," Drew said. "I've been looking for you."

The other man paused before saying, "Looks like you found me." He raised one eyebrow and added, "Think you can keep up?"

Then the Honda peeled out of the parking lot, cutting off an onslaught of traffic.

"Dammit!" Drew stepped on the gas, his backend fishtailing as he made the turn, doing his best to keep close to Xavier's bumper. The Honda took off, weaving in and out of traffic, taking turns too quickly, and recklessly cutting off other cars.

Drew kept a tight hold on the steering wheel, determined

not to lose him this time. But then the Honda took a sharp left turn, and Drew got stuck waiting as a half-dozen big rigs barreled down the road in the opposite direction, cutting off his access. The moment they passed by, Drew gunned it, knowing he'd likely lost Xavier. But to his surprise, the Honda was three streets down, idling at a stop sign.

It was then Drew got suspicious. Why had Xavier been waiting for him in the marina parking lot? And why was he making sure Drew had ample opportunity to follow him? He wasn't seriously trying to shake the deputy sheriff. If he was, he'd have been long gone after making that left turn.

That sixth sense kicked in, and Drew just knew someone was in danger. He didn't know who; all he knew was it was someone he cared about. It was the same feeling he'd had the night Charlotte died and the night his mother had almost lost her life in a car accident.

He glanced over at his phone and said, "Call Noel."

The Bluetooth kicked in, and the sound of her phone ringing blasted from the vehicle's stereo system. She picked up on the second ring. "Hey, Drew. I thought you had to run down a lead in Eureka. Did you learn anything?"

He hesitated. He didn't want to worry her, but he also knew she was skittish in the trust department. "Actually, I'm following him right now."

She let out a gasp. "On foot?"

"No. We're headed south on 101. I don't know what's going on, but it's like he wants me to follow him or something, like he's baiting me. He's had ample opportunity to ditch me."

"Drew, be careful. Call backup. If he's in any way mixed-up in that murder—"

"Don't worry. I'll be cautious. I'm just going to see where he ends up, and then I'll call backup if needed."

"Drew—"

"Listen, Noel, I'm actually calling because I just have this feeling that something isn't right back home. I want to make sure you and Daisy are all right."

"I'm fine. Daisy's still at school. I'm sure she's fine too, otherwise they would've called me. I pick her up in twenty minutes."

Relief rushed through him, but the uneasy feeling was still there. "All right. Just call me after you pick her up, okay?"

"I will. And Drew?"

"Yeah?"

"Make sure you stay safe. I'm not going to tolerate Xavier upending my life again."

"You got it, love." He pressed a button, ending the call, and continued to follow Xavier off the highway and down the back roads of Humboldt county.

Eventually the Honda made it back to town, and after forty-five minutes of driving, Xavier pulled into the parking lot of Pies, Pies, and More Pies.

Drew didn't know what to make of this new turn of events. He parked his SUV near the exit and continued to let the vehicle idle as he waited to see what Xavier would do. The driver's door opened, and Drew tensed. If Xavier had a weapon, anything could happen.

As Xavier's feet hit the asphalt, Drew's left hand tightened around the door handle while his right hand palmed his stun gun. Xavier slammed his door shut at the same time Drew threw his open. Drew jumped out of the SUV, aiming the stun gun in Xavier's direction while using the door as a shield.

He was ready to pull the trigger. But when he peeked over the door at Xavier, he was stunned to find out the driver wasn't Xavier at all. His skin was a few shades darker, and his hair was jet-black.

"What the hell?" Drew glanced at the license plate of the

Honda, quickly confirmed it was Xavier's, then ran over to the guy, stopping him just before he walked into the restaurant. "Where the hell is Xavier?"

"Who?" the guy asked in confusion.

"Xavier... I mean Victor. The guy who is supposed to be driving that vehicle over there." Drew pointed at the Honda, ready to rip someone's head off. He was being played. He knew it was Xavier he'd seen at the marina. The two men had made eye contact. Drew had seen the man's face, one he'd know anywhere as it was almost a mirror of his daughter's. This man must've switched vehicles with Xavier at some point, which meant he'd just been led on a wild goose chase.

"I don't know. That guy who called himself Victor paid me fifty bucks to drive around for forty minutes. He told me to leave the vehicle here when I was done."

"He just paid you fifty bucks to drive, and you did it without question?" Drew asked, his eyes narrowed in suspicion.

"Hey man, I've got an electric bill to pay. Fifty bucks is fifty bucks."

"And you'd never seen him before?"

The man shook his head. "I was coming off a fishing job when he asked if I wanted to make some extra money today. That's all I know."

Drew fumed while the man disappeared into the restaurant. Drew followed, but only to take a look around and see if Xavier was waiting around inside. But as he expected, Xavier was nowhere to be found. Drew retreated and jogged over to the Honda. Inside, he spotted a hat, a scarf, a pair of gloves, and an extra jacket. He was certain he'd seen Xavier wearing the scarf the day he'd walked out of the Sunshine Hotel. If he could get his hands on it, he might be able to track Xavier. But the doors were all locked.

"Damn," Drew muttered. He ran back into the restaurant and forced the man Xavier had hired to drive in his place to accompany him back to the parking lot.

"I have rights," the man said, glaring at Drew.

"You could also be arrested and taken in for questioning. Or you can open that door and hand me that scarf." Drew didn't really have any grounds for arresting the man. There certainly weren't any laws forbidding him from driving around town. Drew hadn't turned his lights on and asked him to pullover. But he could take him in for questioning and would if he refused.

"Fine. Geez. Keep your pants on." The man pulled out a set of keys, and in no time he had the door open.

Drew reached in and grabbed the items of clothing. Now all he needed was a body of water. "Thank you," he told the man then jogged back to his SUV.

The Elk River was close, but the ocean would provide him with more energy. Making a snap decision, Drew hightailed it north to the closest beach. It was a gray Tuesday afternoon and to Drew's relief, the beach was deserted. The less distraction the better. He parked his SUV, grabbed the scarf, and jogged down to the water's edge. Pure energy poured into him from the crashing waves, filling him up, making him hum with the intensity of it.

Drew fell to his knees in the sand, held on to the scarf with both hands, and concentrated on Xavier. The man's face flashed in his mind, clear as day. Then there he was, standing in front of the Keating Hollow elementary school. Drew was frozen in the vision, forced to watch as Xavier held his arms out to Daisy, scooped her up, and holding her close to him in a protective embrace, started to run.

"No!" Drew shouted and took off for his vehicle.

CHAPTER 23

As soon as Noel got off the phone with Drew, she started to get nervous. She wasn't one to discount that nagging feeling. And the fact that Drew was caught up in an investigation that had to do with her ex made her uneasy enough that she grabbed her keys and headed straight for her vehicle. If she had her way, she'd be the first one in the pickup line when school let out. Once she had Daisy safely by her side and Drew was back in town, she'd start to relax again.

"Going to get Daisy," she called to Alec.

He glanced up from his spot behind the check-in counter. "Already?"

"Yeah. I don't want to get caught in the line today." She waved and disappeared out the back door. But when she clicked the key fob to unlock her car door, nothing happened. "Crap," she muttered, adding *get a new battery* to her mental to-do list as she used the key to open the door.

Once she was belted in, she shoved the key into the ignition and… nothing. "No. This isn't happening." She tried again. Nothing. The car was completely dead. "Dammit."

Frustrated, she hopped out of her five-year-old SUV and ran back into the inn. "Alec?"

"Hey, I thought you left," he said.

"My battery is dead. Do you think you could jump it?"

"Sure." He put his pen down and followed her outside. While he positioned his truck next to her vehicle, Noel pulled out the jumper cables. It took a little bit of maneuvering, but eventually they got the cables attached and her SUV running.

"Thank you," she said, relieved as she jumped back into her SUV. "I owe you one."

He waved her off. "Don't even worry about it. It all washes out in the end."

She smiled at him and pulled out of the small lot. When she stopped at the light, she glanced at the clock and gritted her teeth. Jumpstarting her battery had taken longer than she'd thought. School was just getting out, and Daisy could already be waiting for her. While she waited for the light to turn, she checked all her settings to see what could've drained her battery. It didn't take long to realize that her lights had been turned from Auto to On. Noel's hands started to sweat as she gripped the wheel tighter. She never changed the controls. And since she was the only one whoever drove her vehicle, someone else had done that. Had that been on purpose, she wondered?

Had Xavier come to town and purposely sabotaged her vehicle so she couldn't get around? The idea sounded crazy, but so was the fact that he was in Eureka and associated with an unidentifiable dead man. What in the world was her ex up to?

Noel drove a little faster than she should to the school and tried not to lose it when she found herself at the back up the pickup line. All she wanted in that moment was to get her daughter home where she could keep an eye on her.

The line seemed to move slower than molasses, but in reality, Noel knew it was going about as fast as it usually did. She finally rounded the turn, giving her a view of the kids waiting to be picked up.

And the man walking up to the school with his arms wide open.

Xavier.

Noel lowered her window just in time to hear her sweet girl cry, "Daddy!"

"No!" Noel cried, hearing the word echo in her mind as she leaped out of the car.

Daisy flung herself into Xavier's arms. He scooped her up, holding her tightly.

"Put my daughter down right this minute," Noel demanded, wind kicking up around her as if it had a will of its own. The leaves in the trees rustled angrily. A trash can fell to its side and rolled. Kids let out startled cries, surprised by the rush of power streaming from her.

"Noel, stop!" Xavier ordered as he ran to her, Daisy clutched in his arms. "Rein in your magic. No one is taking Daisy."

She didn't believe him. Why else was he there? "Hand her over."

"No." Daisy buried her face into his shoulder, holding on with everything she had. "I don't want to leave Daddy."

Noel stood on the sidewalk in front of the elementary school, heartbroken, and completely pissed-off. "What do you think you're doing?" she asked him as she pried her daughter out of his arms. "You're breaking her heart. You know that, right?"

"No, Mommy, no. I want Daddy," Daisy whimpered, wrapping her legs around her mother while simultaneously trying to reach for him again.

"Noel, please," he said. "Let me explain."

"Are you insane?" She whispered angrily. "I can't believe you did this. Where did you think you were going to take her?"

"Nowhere," he said, holding his hands up and taking a step back. "I just wanted to see you both."

"So you came here? Are you out of your mind?" She stalked over to one of the teachers who was headed straight for them. After apologizing and briefly explaining the situation, she stalked back to her car and got Daisy situated in the back seat. Her daughter reached for her dad and whimpered the entire time. Once Daisy was buckled in, she kissed her on the cheek and tried to soothe her with comforting words, but nothing was going to calm her down, and Noel knew it.

Noel turned to Xavier, who was hovering. "Get in the car. If you try anything or say anything to upset my daughter further, I'll castrate you, got it?"

He nodded once and hurried to get in the vehicle before she changed her mind. And she almost did. Everything inside of her wanted to pull him out of her SUV and kick the crap out of him. How dare he show up at Daisy's school like this. How dare he try to see her without talking to Noel first. He had some balls.

Noel fumed the entire way back to the inn. Once they were out of the car, she grabbed Daisy's hand and jerked her head at Xavier, indicating he should follow. But instead of going inside, she led the way around the back and settled into one of the patio chairs while he sat in the porch swing. Daisy flung herself at him and snuggled in close.

The scene was almost unbearable for Noel to watch. She turned her head and shivered in the cool afternoon air. If she was cold, she knew Daisy must be freezing. She waved a hand, instantly warming the air around them.

"Your magic is stronger now," Xavier said.

She shrugged. "It always is when I'm angry."

"Right… I didn't mean any harm," Xavier said, wrapping his arm around his daughter.

"Is that why you sabotaged my vehicle? It was clever of you to make it look like a mistake," she said, her tone dripping with sarcasm.

"What do you mean sabotage your vehicle?" His brow was wrinkled in confusion. "Didn't you just drive it to the school?"

"The battery was dead, Xavier. Are you seriously denying that you somehow turned the lights on?"

He glanced away and tapped his foot nervously as he said, "I just wanted a little time to say goodbye."

"You're something else, you know that? Couldn't you have just asked me? Or were you too afraid of what I'd say?" She wanted to slug him. If he hadn't been holding Daisy, she might not have held back. "I bet you're the one who kept calling the inn and hanging up on me."

He sucked in a breath but didn't answer her. She took that as a yes. Noel hated that Daisy was present for the conversation she couldn't put off. She and her ex had things to discuss, and most of them weren't suitable for Daisy's ears. "Where are you headed this time, Xavier?"

"South, I think."

"South, you think?" Noel sighed. "Daisy, sweetheart?"

Her daughter lifted her head and peered at her mother.

"I need you to go check on Buffy. Can you do that for me?"

"But Daddy's here. I don't want to go," she said, barely holding back a whimper.

"Daddy and I need to discuss some grown-up things, sweetheart. I know you miss him, but we need a few minutes. I promise you he won't leave before you get to spend some time together."

"But I don't want you to leave," she said, looking up at him with tears in her eyes.

"I know, sweet pea. I don't have a choice, but I won't leave without saying goodbye." His expression was so loving and gentle, but all it did was manage to piss Noel off further. Where had that man been all this time?

Reluctantly, Daisy slid off the swing. She dragged her feet and glared at her mother until she turned the corner and disappeared out of sight. A few moments later, they heard the back door open and slam shut.

Silence fell between them. Noel just stared at him, waiting for him to say whatever it was he came to say.

He cleared his throat. "I need to apologize."

"Yes, you do," she said, crossing her arms over her chest. "But not to me. To your daughter."

"To both of you," he insisted.

She let out a huff. "It's wasted on me, Xavier. Nothing you say is going to make this right."

He grimaced as he nodded his agreement. "I know. But I'm still sorry. So very sorry for the way that this all went down."

She blinked. "Sorry for the way it went down? Not sorry for leaving?"

"Of course, I'm sorry for leaving. But I didn't have a choice. I had to. Otherwise..." He ran a hand through his thick hair. When he glanced back up, his green eyes were pleading with her. "There is so much to explain. I didn't want to leave. I had to. Please, Noel, just listen while I get this out."

"Fine. I'm listening." Her tone was short and full of skepticism. Nothing he could say would make this better, but she couldn't deny that she was intensely curious. Just where the hell had he been, and why had he left so abruptly?

"There are things you don't know about my past," he said.

"Clearly."

"I meant my past before we met." He leaned forward and glanced away again.

"You told me you grew up in Oregon," she said. "You were an only child, and your parents died in a car accident."

He turned back to her. "None of that is true."

She couldn't say she was surprised. His past was nonexistent. There had to be a reason why it vanished from all viable records. "I'm listening."

Xavier stared her straight in the eye and spit it out. "I grew up in a crime family."

Honestly, it was what she'd been expecting to hear. How could she not when his past had been all but erased? But it was still a gut-punch that made it hard to breathe. Finally, she forced out, "Are you still a participant?"

"Not a willing one."

She closed her eyes, not sure she wanted to hear anything else. "In that case, you should probably leave. It's not safe for Daisy." Or him for that matter. If Drew happened to show up, things would not go well for Xavier.

"I will, but there are things to say first," he said.

"Then you better just lay it out there."

He did just that. Xavier explained how he'd been forced to be a drug runner for his uncle from the time he'd been eight years old. As a teenager, he'd been there when his uncle executed three rival drug dealers and forced one of the leader's daughter to join their crew. He'd taken an interest in her and tried to force her to be his girlfriend. Xavier had helped her escape before anything could escalate, and that's when he left and never looked back. He'd managed to find an earth witch who was skilled at manipulating technology and had paid him an obscene amount of money to make him disappear. Shortly after that, he'd landed in Keating Hollow, hoping to lead a normal life. Then he'd met Noel.

"So, you went on the straight and narrow. Good for you. Except I deserved to know about your past *before* we got married and started a family, don't you think?"

He nodded. "Yes. But I was desperate to put the past behind me. I never had any intention of returning to that life."

"Yet, you did. I guess I can thank you for not involving me and Daisy."

Pain flashed in his green eyes, and the man just looked gutted. "That's why I left, Noel. They found me."

She sucked in a sharp breath, pain radiating from somewhere deep in her soul. He hadn't left them because he stopped caring. He'd left to protect them. "Why didn't you tell me?" she whispered.

"I didn't want you anywhere near any of that, Noel. Why would I want that for you and Daisy?"

"But... we loved you."

He slid off the swing and dropped to his knees in front of her, grabbing her hands. "I never stopped loving you both. Never."

She stared down at their connected hands and knew she couldn't say the same. The love she'd felt for him had turned to resentment and something close to hatred. She wasn't proud of that fact, but after watching her daughter suffer so many nights because she missed her dad, she just hadn't been able to forgive. Maybe now, with answers, she could find a way forward. "Where have you been all these years?"

He tightened his grip on her hands, closed his eyes, and said, "I don't really know. Not long after I left here, I was drugged, force-fed a potion that left me with no memories."

Holy balls. This was just getting worse and worse. "And now? What happened?"

He shook his head. "I don't know exactly. Some of it's coming back to me, but it's fuzzy, to be honest. Victor stole my identity because I had no record. He was also the one feeding me that potion. Then he showed up dead, and I came back to myself. As my memories started to come back, I ended up here. You should know... I saw Daisy last week."

"You what?" She pulled her hands out of his, ready to spit fire.

"Please, Noel. I wasn't fully myself yet. I didn't understand. All I knew was that there was something... someone here that I needed to see. I showed up, saw her, and a flood of memories came roaring back. I thought she might've seen me, but I wasn't sure. I was so confused. I took off so I could sort it all out."

She suddenly started to feel overwhelmed. His story was fantastical and almost unbelievable. But at the same time, she knew he was telling the truth. She could feel it in her gut. "Is that the only time you were here in town before today?"

He shook his head. "After I sorted out my memories, I came back here. I wanted to see you, talk to you, explain. But..."

"But?" Her heart was hammering against her ribcage.

"I saw you with the town cop." He moved back to the swing and stared at the ground. "I knew I could never talk to you when he was around, so I waited until the time was right."

"Until you could send him on a wild goose chase?" she filled in.

He nodded. "If your boyfriend hauls me in, there's no doubt I'll end up incarcerated. I'm pretty sure all of Victor's crimes are going to fall on my head. I need time to sort it out."

"And when you do?"

"I've already decided I'm going to the authorities. I can't live this life. I want what we had before, Noel. That was all I ever wanted."

She stared at him, her heart broken. Then she shook her head. "I can't go back, Xavier. Not now. Probably not ever. You lied to me. You left me. But more importantly, you didn't trust me. And Daisy…" A small sob got caught in her throat. "She's suffered because we were blindsided. I'm sorry, but I can't be a part of that again."

Deep sadness radiated from him, but he stood and nodded. "I understand. Can I say goodbye to my daughter?"

"Of course." Noel disappeared into the inn to retrieve Daisy.

Her daughter had been sitting against the door, her arms wrapped around her knees while she silently cried.

"Come on, sweetheart. Your dad is waiting," Noel said.

Daisy bolted out the door and back into her father's arms.

CHAPTER 24

DREW SPED down the two-lane road heading into Keating Hollow, taking the turns too fast and passing anyone and everyone who got in his way. He'd tried to call Noel no less than six times. Every single call went straight to voicemail. He'd even tried calling the inn, but he'd run into the same thing. Voicemail.

Where the hell was everyone?

Then he'd called Clay and asked him to check on his girls. Unfortunately, Clay was meeting with a supplier in Eureka and was even further away.

He tightened his grip on the steering wheel and headed straight for the school. It was deserted. He hadn't really expected anyone to still be there and kept moving. Finally, he pulled into the small parking lot behind her inn. He took off, running for the door, but before he disappeared inside, he heard a cry come from the side of the building. Drew immediately switched course and followed the sounds of an upset little girl.

He rounded the corner and spotted Xavier standing with

his back to Drew in the middle of the patio area. Daisy was in his arms, crying, "No, Daddy, no. No."

Rage filled him. How dare Xavier come to Keating Hollow after deliberately distracting Drew so that he could terrorize his little girl. He wouldn't be doing that ever again. Not on Drew's watch. "Xavier Anderson, let Daisy go, now!"

Xavier put Daisy down and turned around to face Drew.

"Daisy, come here, baby," Noel said and grabbed her daughter's hand, yanking her into her arms just as soon as she had a hold on her.

"Take Daisy inside, Noel. I'll handle this from here," Drew said.

"Drew, I—"

"Please, Noel. Go now," he pleaded, glancing at her child. If things went south with Xavier, he did not want it to happen in front of Daisy.

"Right. But please, try to be reasonable," she said and then disappeared around the side of the inn.

"You made a mistake coming back here, Anderson," Drew said, palming his stun gun.

"Why's that, Baker?" he asked with a sneer. "Is it because you finally found the balls to move in on my family?"

"Big talk from a man who deserted them."

"You know nothing about me," Xavier said, glaring at him.

"I know enough. Now put your hands up. I'm taking you in."

"The hell you are. I was just here to say goodbye. Now I'm out of here."

"Move one inch, and I swear to god I'll drop you in two seconds flat. Understand?"

"What's the matter, Baker? Are you smarting because you spent all day driving around Eureka with nothing to show for it?"

Drew glared at Xavier, unwilling to take his bait. "I'm going to count to three. If you don't comply, I'm going to drop you on your ass, got it?"

Xavier snorted out a laugh. "Go ahead and try it and see where that gets you with my *wife*."

"*Ex-wife*," Drew corrected.

Xavier shrugged, then turned and started to walk away.

"This is your last warning, Anderson. Stop now, or I'm pulling this trigger."

"Do what you have to do, Baker," he said.

"You asked for it," Drew said.

"Drew, don't," Noel said from behind him.

But it was too late. Drew had already pulled the trigger on his stun gun. Xavier fell to his knees then flat on his face.

"Drew! What have you done?" Noel asked in a harsh whisper.

He glanced back at her, somewhat surprised by the anger he saw shining back at him.

"Just my job, Noel. What did you expect me to do?"

"Do you feel better now?"

He glanced up at her. "Honestly, yes."

She narrowed her eyes at him and shook her head, looking disappointed and tired. "There are things you don't know."

"I'm certain that's true." Drew moved to Xavier's side, and stared down at him dispassionately. "You'll never hurt them again, got it?"

Xavier blinked once, as if to acknowledge Drew's statement. Then Drew got to work. Twenty minutes later, he had Xavier Anderson locked up in the town's single cell and had alerted Sheriff Barnes.

~

"You don't understand," Noel said. She was standing in Drew's office, hands on her hips, glaring at him.

"I think I do," he said, trying to sound as reasonable as possible. "You're telling me he was part of a crime family for years, and yet you think I should've just let him go."

"That is not what I'm saying," she insisted. "I'm saying that you didn't need to hit him with that stun gun."

"He was leaving, Noel. It was the safest course of action for everyone."

"I'm not sure I share your opinion," she said, her tone heated. "He was only here to say goodbye to Daisy. You didn't need to zap him."

"You don't know that." Drew stood up and pressed his hands against his desk. "In fact, you barely know anything about him. Everything he said could be a lie."

"I know him, Drew. He wasn't lying to me. He loved us and was trying to do what was best for us. That has to count for something."

Drew just stared at her, wondering where this person had come from. Had it really only taken one conversation with the man who'd ripped her heart out and stomped on it for her to forgive him for all she'd been through? "What's this really about?"

"What?" Her brow creased in confusion. "I don't know what you're trying to say."

"Do you still love him? Are you thinking now that he's apologized maybe there's something to salvage there? Because I really don't understand."

She gaped at him, and he suppressed a wince. Clearly that was the wrong thing to say. "You can't be serious," she said.

He ground his teeth together. "What am I supposed to think? He's a self-professed criminal, and you're pissed-off because I wouldn't just let him walk. I don't understand what you wanted me to do. I can't *not* do my job."

She stared at him, disappointment in her pretty blue eyes. Then she moved toward his closed door. She paused, glanced back, and said, "All I wanted you to do was listen."

He opened his mouth to respond, but she walked out and quietly closed the door behind her.

CHAPTER 25

THREE DAYS HAD PASSED since Drew had hauled Xavier off to jail. And it'd been three days since Noel had talked to him. He'd texted to ask when they could get together, and she'd told him she needed some time. She'd wanted to focus on Daisy.

What she hadn't expected was that Daisy seemed to be doing perfectly fine. It was as if seeing Xavier and hearing him tell her how much he loved her and hadn't wanted to leave had somehow soothed her fears. Sure, she'd been upset that he'd left, but Noel could see that some sort of switch had flipped in her daughter. Her dad had come back for her, and that was what she'd needed.

It didn't hurt that they'd been able to go into Eureka and visit him. Noel hadn't made the decision lightly. She didn't want to do anything that would hurt Daisy further, but Daisy's therapist had said it would probably do her good to know that he hadn't just disappeared again. So she steeled herself and made the trip. Daisy had been subdued on the ride into town but was happy enough on the way back home. As hurt as Noel had been that Xavier hadn't trusted her and had lied by omission, she didn't feel right about keeping Daisy from him completely. She had a right to know her father.

The truth was she felt sorry for Xavier. It wasn't his fault he'd grown up in a terrible family situation. And he had tried to leave. The entire time she'd known him, he'd never given any indication that he was anything other than a law-abiding citizen.

"What are you going to do if Xavier finds a way out of this mess, Noel?" Her younger sister Faith asked her as she deftly arranged her blond hair into a French braid.

The four sisters were sitting at Yvette's kitchen table, going over the plans for Abby's upcoming wedding.

Noel shrugged. "That largely depends on him, I guess. I want Daisy to be able to spend time with him. No matter his faults, he was a good dad."

Abby glanced up from her wedding planning books. "She means, what are you going to do about Drew?"

Noel frowned. "What does Drew have to do with Xavier?"

"Aren't you two dating?" Faith asked.

Were they? Noel wasn't sure where they stood at the moment. They certainly hadn't broken up, but then they hadn't had a chance to speak yet either. "I guess so. We had a little bit of a falling out, so we'll have to see what happens."

Abby scooted over and covered Noel's hand with hers. "We're just worried you might be tempted to get back together with Xavier."

Noel blinked. "What gave you that idea?"

"Because he was your first love," Abby said matter-of-factly.

"And he's the father of your child," Yvette added.

"We're just worried about you," Faith said.

"First love?" Noel let out a small huff of laughter. "Is that what you guys think?"

"Isn't he?" Faith said.

Noel shook her head. "No. Actually, the first man I fell in love with was Drew."

All three of her sisters sat back with stunned expressions on their faces. Finally, Abby cleared her throat. "Are you saying you never loved Xavier or that you and Drew had a thing at some point that no one knew about?"

Noel smiled patiently. "Remember that summer I was a camp counselor?"

Yvette and Faith nodded.

"Was I already in New Orleans?" Abby asked.

"Yes. Drew was there too, and we didn't date, but we came close. And we were best friends. I fell completely and utterly head over heels for him that summer. I think it's fair to say he had feelings for me, too, but he was still in so much pain from Charlotte's death that the timing was all wrong. When the summer was over, we went our separate ways. We were still friendly, but Drew always kept his distance. It took him a long time to put her death behind him. I don't think having feelings for a Townsend helped."

"Noel," Abby said on a whisper. "I'm so sorry. That must've been really hard."

"Mostly because you weren't here," Noel said quietly as she stared at her mug.

Abby's fingers tightened on her sister's. When Noel finally looked at her, Abby's eyes were brimming with tears. "I'm sorry," she said. "You know I missed you, too. More than I think you realize. I just… I was very much like Drew. Caught up in my own pain. You have no idea how glad I am to be back here with you three. I missed so much of your lives."

"It's water under the bridge now. I'm sorry I didn't come to see you," Noel said, meaning it. If she'd just reached out to Abby, not let her walls cement in place, maybe things would've been different. "We have a lot to catch up on."

Abby's smile wobbled as she nodded. All of the pain and frustration of the past years had finally fallen away after the pact they'd made in Abby's bedroom. Now they just needed to find their footing again.

"Okay, enough about Noel's drama." Yvette gave her a gentle smile. "I spoke to Isaac yesterday."

All three of her sisters turned and gave her their undivided attention.

"And?" Noel asked.

"I'm still angry, but at least I don't hate him anymore," she said. "He came over and apologized and asked if we could talk, so I let him in. The long and short of it is he fell in love with Jake. He said that he kind of always knew that he was attracted to men, but that he loved me so much he thought he could just ignore it. Then Jake came along. He said he truly didn't want it to happen, but it just did. Guys, he told me he's ashamed of himself."

"Because he cheated on you?" Abby asked. "He should be. That's not at all okay."

"No. I mean, yes, he's ashamed of his behavior and for not being honest with me, but he meant he was ashamed that he had feelings for another man."

"What did you say?" Noel asked.

She sighed. "I told him that he needed to be true to himself. And then I told him that I'd love him no matter what and that he shouldn't be ashamed." Tears glistened in her dark eyes. "It breaks my heart that he feels that way."

"You're a good person, Vette," Abby said.

"She's right," Faith added. "It must've been difficult to support him considering how much he hurt you."

"He didn't want to. I believe him. I'm just heartbroken. But I don't want him to live a lie either," Yvette said.

Noel pushed a plate of cookies toward her sister. "Today we

can eat our feelings. Tomorrow, maybe we can find a way to be friends with our exes."

Yvette nodded. "I don't want to lose him in my life. But I do need some time."

"Does that mean you forgive, Xavier?" Faith asked Noel.

"Yes," she said, meaning it. "But we're never going to be a couple again. As it turns out, I'm in love with someone else."

Abby pressed her hand to her heart. "You are? In love?"

"Yeah." Noel fiddled with one of the cookies. "But who knows where we go from here."

"You just need to talk to him," Faith said. "I'm sure you can work it out."

"Definitely," Abby added. "Clay and I saw him last night. He looked miserable. Put the man out of his misery, Noel. He was just trying to protect you and Daisy. He loves her, too, you know."

Noel nodded. She did know. She hadn't forgotten that he'd driven like a bat out of hell back to town, left her half a dozen messages she hadn't gotten until later, and called Clay for help when he'd thought Xavier was snatching her child. He'd have moved heaven and earth to keep her safe. "I'll talk to him later... after we get this wedding stuff done."

Abby cheered, and they all laughed. Then she asked, "What do you think about the bride and groom arriving to the reception in a tricked-out golf cart?"

CHAPTER 26

DREW PACED HIS OFFICE. He'd just gotten off the phone with the sheriff over in Eureka and learned that everything Xavier had told Noel had been true. After they'd checked out his story, they'd found a hidden compound up north near Crescent City where Xavier's family had been running illegal drugs for the last five years, and that they'd used Lilies and More and the Moon River Inn to launder their drug money. Prior to that, they'd had a home base down in Fresno before law enforcement had turned up the heat, forcing them to relocate.

And more importantly, it turned out that Victor Franks—the man who'd stolen Xavier's identity—had been murdered by a rival drug pusher. Xavier hadn't had anything to do with it. For the last three years, Xavier had been a victim, and he wouldn't be held accountable for any crimes he'd committed as long as he turned state's evidence. It was a big deal and a huge win for the state.

He strode out of his office. "I'm going out for a while, Clarissa."

"Deputy Baker—" she said.

"Not now. I have something important to take care of." He reached for the front door but froze when he heard her voice.

"Drew?"

"Noel?" He turned around and blinked to make sure he wasn't hallucinating. Had she been standing there the entire time?

"I don't want to keep you, but if you have time later—" she started.

"I have time now." He strode over, placed his hand on the small of her back, and led her into his office without saying a word to Clarissa.

"It's really okay if you have somewhere to be," she said the moment he closed the door.

He shook his head and guided her to the couch against the far wall. "I was headed to see you. I have news."

Her eyebrows shot up. "What kind of news?"

"I just got off the phone with the sheriff over in Eureka. Xavier has been cleared of the murder of the John Doe."

She nodded but didn't look surprised. "That's good."

"And he's turning state's evidence. He won't serve any time for his past deeds and will even be assigned protection, if that's deemed necessary. Though I doubt it will be. They think they got everyone in his family's crime ring."

"I'm glad to hear that," she said, giving nothing away.

He gazed at her, trying to judge where she was at with all of this. Where she was at with him. There was only one way to find out. "Listen, Noel. I think I owe you an apology."

She frowned and opened her mouth to respond, but before she could speak, he cut her off.

"That day when your ex sent me on a wild goose chase, I was certain he was going to harm Daisy. I understand now that he was just trying to keep me occupied so that he could talk to you two without my interference, but I didn't know that at the time. And when I saw that vision of him and Daisy, I lost it. I'm sure that played into my reaction when I saw him with you guys."

"I imagine it did," she said, watching him intently.

"I just..." He sucked in a deep breath and sat on the couch beside her, taking her hands in his. "I owe you an apology. I was on edge that day, but you were right, I should've taken the time to listen to you. I'm sorry if I made it seem like your opinion wasn't important. Because it is very important. And I guess I have to admit that some of my insecurity was showing. We've just found our way back together. I don't want to lose you or Daisy."

Noel stared at him for a moment. Then tears filled her eyes and fell silently down her cheeks.

"Noel, I—don't cry." Hell, what had he done? He reached up and gently wiped the tears away, unsure what else to say.

"I'm sorry, too," she finally said, blinking back the tears. "I know you were just doing your job. That you were just protecting us. It was a stressful day. Daisy... well, you know she's had anxiety issues since her dad left the first time. I had no idea how all that would affect her."

"You don't need to apologize to me, Noel," he said gently. "How is Daisy doing with all of this?"

She let out a small bark of laughter. "Surprisingly, better than the rest of us. She's thrilled he came back and seems to be taking it all in stride. We saw him yesterday in Eureka. I'm pretty sure he's going to stick around Keating Hollow, assuming everything works out with his legal issues."

"What does that mean for you guys?" Drew asked cautiously. His heart was in his throat. If she'd decided she needed to try to repair her family, that was it for him. He'd be the odd man out, and rightly so. Family was too important. He wouldn't try to change her mind.

She shrugged. "I guess it means custody agreements and visitation schedules. I want Daisy to have a relationship with her dad."

A small kernel of hope blossomed in his chest. "And you? Do you want a relationship with him?"

She gave him a gentle smile and pressed a soft hand to his stubbled cheek. "Only one that revolves around Daisy. I want to be a responsible co-parent, but as far as anything else between me and Xavier… it's not in the cards. My heart belongs to another."

"But it used to belong to him," Drew said, wanting to get it all out on the table. "And the three of you were a family. It's not too late to repair that."

She dropped her hand and narrowed her eyes at him. "Are you trying to tell me you want out of this relationship we've started, Drew? Because if you are, just be clear about it."

It was his turn to laugh. But there was no humor in it. "Not at all, Noel. I'm so far in with you, you're the only thing I've thought about since I saw you last. I've been in such a bad mood that Clarissa threatened to lock me in the jail cell until I figure out how to be civil. I just want to put all the cards out on the table. If you think you might want to try again with Xavier, then I need to know now, because I won't—can't—stand in the way of that. But please, tell me now and let me get on with grieving what we could've had. It would be easier on all of us."

Noel got to her feet and started to pace, seeming to consider what he'd just said.

Drew leaned forward and clasped his hands together, waiting for her to speak and end his torture.

Finally, she stopped, placed her hands on her hips, and said, "You're something else, you know that?"

There wasn't any heat in her tone, but still, he didn't know if that was a good thing or a bag thing. He just shrugged.

"Drew," she said, crouching down in front of him. "There are a few things that I need to clear up." She placed her hands over his. "You know my mom left us when I was ten years old, right? Just up and left us and never came back."

"Yeah. I knew that," he said, nodding.

"You also know how much that betrayal affected me, right?"

"Sure."

Noel shifted and took a seat next to him. "Now imagine how I'd feel when my husband, who also knew that information and knew how deeply it hurt me, up and did the exact same thing. Just left. No note. No explanation. No goodbye. Add in the fact that I had to watch my young daughter, who loved him with all her heart, suffer the consequences. Do you think I'd be able to forgive him, no matter what his reasons were?"

"He was trying to protect you. You know that, right?" Drew asked, wondering why he was defending the man. He supposed he just needed to know that she was completely sure she was done with him.

"I'm not a fragile piece of glass, Drew. He could've—no should've—told me about his past. Even if leaving was the best option, I deserved to know why."

She has a very good point, he thought. "So, no forgiveness, then?"

"Oh, I can forgive him. I just can't be with someone who doesn't see me as an equal partner and who isn't honest about who and what they are. I understand why he did what he did, but I can't go back. What happened can't be changed. And I've moved on. I'm all-in with the deputy sheriff, unless this is all too much for him. If it is, he needs to let me know."

The dread that Drew had been carrying around with him for the last three days vanished as a slow smile claimed his lips. He raised one hand, cupping her neck, and said, "It's definitely not too much for him."

"Good," she said. "Now kiss me."

CHAPTER 27

NOEL STOOD to the left of the wedding arbor, waiting for her sister to make her way down the aisle. It was New Year's Eve, and most of the residents of Keating Hollow had gathered at Lin's orchard to witness the nuptials of Clay and Abby.

The Townsend sisters had outdone themselves getting the orchard ready for the festivities. Yvette had created hundreds of floating candles that made the space glow in soft light. Faith, being a water witch, had created a half-dozen moving portraits of Abby, Clay, and Olive, all made out of water and depicting their happy life together. Noel's gift was more practical. Being that is was December, she'd created a giant bubble of protection to keep the wind from ruining the outdoor event. It wasn't flashy, but it was priceless, considering they'd rejected the idea of an indoor wedding. Abby and Clay were both earth witches, and they very much wanted to commit to each other in the outdoors, with nature surrounding them.

Everything else was simple and beautiful. Rose, lavender, and thyme bundles adorned the arbor, while clear twinkle lights lit up the nearby orchard. Noel glanced past Clay, who was waiting for his bride to walk down the aisle, and she made eye contact with Drew. He was watching her with awe in his handsome face. She smiled at him and blew him a kiss. The last few weeks had been nothing short of magical.

Xavier had promised to cooperate with the authorities and had moved to Keating Hollow. He'd gotten his own place and started spending a lot of time with Daisy. The two were like peas in a pod, falling into an easy rapport with each other as if no time had passed. She hadn't had one nightmare since Xavier's return. Noel still had her daughter seeing a therapist occasionally, just to be on the safe side, but even the therapist was making noise about stopping the appointments unless something came up.

On the nights that Daisy spent with Xavier, Noel spent hers with Drew. And as a bonus, Noel felt better than ever. Her energy levels were up, and she knew it was because of Drew. The man just made her happy. She suspected it was only a matter of time until she and Drew were the ones planning a wedding, but they had to give Daisy time to adjust.

Noel was still making goo-goo eyes at Drew when she heard Bruno Mars singing "Marry You." She glanced up and laughed when she spotted Wanda chauffeuring Abby in her golf cart to the end of the aisle. Wanda pulled the vehicle to a stop and killed the music.

The real wedding song, "Lucky" by Jason Mraz, started to play. Olive and Daisy hopped out of the cart with flower baskets in hand, and together the pair tossed rose petals as they skipped down the aisle. It was the most adorable thing Noel had ever seen.

Then everything seemed to stop, and all eyes were on Abby. She stood with their dad, bright and glowing with love, her eyes never leaving Clay's.

Noel's heart swelled, and she thought it would burst right

then and there. Her sister deserved this happiness, and Clay and Olive did, too. Noel clutched her bouquet as silent tears streamed down her cheeks while she watched her sister, her best friend, marry the man of her dreams.

~

"COME SIT WITH US," Drew said, pulling Noel away from one of Clay's second cousins. He'd apparently taken a liking to her and wouldn't take no for an answer.

"Got to go. Remember the boyfriend I was talking about?" Noel said to the inebriated man. "This is him."

Boon, Clay's cousin from Nevada, swept his gaze over Drew and said, "I can take him."

Drew laughed. "I'd like to see you try, man."

"Lay off, Boon," Clay said, coming up from behind them. "That's my best man and his girl. He's also the town lawman, so watch it."

Boon grumbled something about needing to find another bridesmaid to hook up with and wandered off.

"Good luck with that," Noel said, laughing. The other two bridesmaids were Yvette, who was entirely too uptight for a one-night-stand, and Faith, who was entirely too sweet for one.

"He'll likely pass out at the table before he gets another word out," Drew said, watching the guy stumble away.

Noel nodded. He was a fair mess.

"Come on," Drew said. "Daisy here has something to ask you."

Noel glanced down at her daughter. "You do? What's that?"

"This way, Mommy." Daisy took her by the hand and led her to a table in the far corner where it was a little bit quieter.

Daisy pointed to a chair with a small box sitting in the middle of a cake plate. "You sit here."

Noel gave her a questioning look but did as she said.

"Drew, you here," she pointed to the chair next to Noel. Once he sat, she climbed up into his lap. His arm went around her waist, steadying her, and the action seemed so natural, it was as if they'd been sitting together like that their whole lives.

Tears stung the backs of Noel's eyes as she gazed at the two people she loved most.

"Go ahead," Drew whispered into Daisy's ear. "Ask her."

Daisy gave her mother a shy smile before turning away. "You ask her," she told Drew.

"Oh no, you don't," he said with a laugh. "You're the one who started this. Go on. Ask her."

Noel frowned, looking between them and the box. "What's going on?"

"Mommy," Daisy said, "didn't Aunt Abby look beautiful?"

"She sure did, baby. Did you tell her that?"

"Not yet," Daisy said.

"Make sure you do before we leave tonight, okay?"

Daisy nodded, paused, took a deep breath, and asked, "When will you and Drew get married?"

"What?" Noel jerked back, stunned. Then she narrowed her eyes at Drew and asked, "Did you put her up to this?"

"Oh, no." He raised one hand as if swearing an oath. "She asked me the same thing twenty minutes ago."

"And what did you say?" she demanded, both intensely curious and mildly horrified she was being put on the spot by Drew and her six-year-old.

"I said just as soon as you were ready." He gave her a self-satisfied smile, and if he hadn't been holding her daughter, she might've seriously considered gut-punching him. Or kissing him. She wasn't sure which.

She turned her attention to her daughter, determined to understand where this question was coming from. Was it just because they were at Abby's wedding, or was this coming from someone else? Someone like Abby, who seemed to think that since she and Clay had tied the knot that everyone should be doing it. "Why do you want me to marry Drew?"

Daisy gave her mom a bright smile. "You'd look really pretty in a wedding dress."

Noel chuckled. "Okay, maybe if it was the right wedding dress. But that's not a good enough reason to get married."

Daisy glanced over at Olive, who was sitting between Abby and Clay at another table. She was holding both their hands and beaming like she'd won the lottery, and Noel began to understand.

"Do you want what Olive has, sweetheart?"

Daisy shook her head, and in a very small voice, she said, "Olive has two mommies. I want two daddies." She glanced back at Drew. "But only if my second daddy is Drew."

Drew's eyes got misty as he hugged Daisy to his chest and whispered, "Sweet girl, nothing would make me happier."

Noel's heart melted right there at that table in her dad's orchard. What was she going to do with that? She met Drew's eyes and realized through her blurred vision that both of them were crying. She sniffed and started to laugh. "Looks like we both got gut-punched by a six-year-old."

"Huh?" Daisy asked, confused.

"Never mind, baby," Noel said, reaching for her daughter. "Don't you worry. When the time is right, I'm sure Drew and I will get married. Until then, let's not rush anything. Okay?"

Daisy frowned and stared at the box in front of them. Then she glanced back at her mom and said, "When you do, can we drive in on the golf cart? That was fun!"

"Anything you want, you little troublemaker. Now go on

and dance with your cousin." She pointed to where Olive was wiggling around on the temporary dancefloor. "Drew and I will be out there in a second."

Daisy's eyes lit up when she spotted Olive, and a second later, she was shaking her hips and waving her arms in time with her new cousin.

Noel turned to Drew with one eyebrow raised. "You helped with that little ambush."

"You're right. I did. And I'm not even sorry," he said, grinning at her.

She shook her head. "You're trouble. You know that?"

He reached out and grabbed the box they'd been tactfully ignoring. "I think it's time you opened this."

She glanced down, then back to him, her mouth suddenly dry. "Is that what I think it is?"

"You'll have to open it to find out."

"Drew—"

"Just open it," he insisted.

Shaking her head, she pulled the top off the white box. Inside, she found a sapphire ring on a silver chain.

"It's the promise ring my dad gave my mother just one month after they started dating," Drew said, taking it from her and fastening it around her neck. "They've been married for forty years this spring."

Noel reached up and fingered the ring. "Are you sure you didn't put Daisy up to that conversation?"

He laughed and shook his head. "Never in a million years would I think to coach her into that. I had already planned on giving this to you tonight." He sat back down, facing her. "I want you to know that I fully intend on marrying you when you're ready... when Daisy's ready, and not just when she's excited about weddings. This is my promise that I'm never letting either of you go again."

Those damn tears were back again, and this time, Noel couldn't stop them.

"I love you, Noel Townsend. One day, I'm going to stand up there at that alter and make you my wife."

"I love you, too Andrew Baker," she said. "Just don't make me wait too long."

"Count on it." Drew leaned in, brushing his lips over hers. "How's Valentine's Day?"

She giggled. "You'll probably have to run it by Daisy."

He glanced over at the little girl who was busy eating yet another piece of wedding cake. "I'm pretty sure as long as it involves chocolate and a pretty dress, she's going to be a solid yes."

"You're probably right," Noel said, grinning as she stood up and held her hand out to him. "You know what they say, like mother like daughter."

He gave her a curious look.

She laughed and tugged him out of his chair. "It's time for cake."

CHAPTER 28

YVETTE TOWNSEND GRABBED a glass of champagne and made her way to an empty table. Clay and Abby had just run off to spend their first night together as a married couple. And now she was hanging out while the rest of their guests celebrated New Year's Eve.

The evening had almost been too much for her. She'd smiled until she was sure her face was going to crack. Just weeks ago, she'd been looking forward to this wedding celebration. She loved weddings... or used to, until her own marriage blew up because of an accountant named Jake.

Now she was doing her damnedest to not rain on her sister's parade. She was thrilled for Abby, but her own heart was still bruised.

"Yvette?" a familiar male voice said from behind her.

She closed her eyes and tried to pretend she hadn't heard her soon-to-be ex-husband or the regret in his tone. Why had he come? Abby and Clay had asked her if they should send him an invitation. In a moment of weakness, she'd said yes. She didn't want him to be ostracized because he'd been too scared to face who he really was for the last twenty years. But now that he was here, all she wanted to do was scream at him. Or punch him. Maybe both. She wasn't mad that he was gay. She was hurt because he'd been her best friend and he'd left her.

"Vette?" he repeated apprehensively.

Not wanting to cause a scene, she turned around and faced him. Damn, he was handsome. Had he lost weight? And was that a new suit? And his freakin' skin even glowed. Isaac looked better than ever, and Yvette knew she looked like she could use a week at the spa. "Hello, Isaac. It was nice of you to come."

"You're not upset that I'm here?" he asked, taking a seat next to her.

Yes. "No. Of course not. Clay is your friend and Abby is still your sister in law. You should be here."

He placed his hand over hers, and she had to fight to not yank hers away. "Thank you for being so understanding."

Understanding. Right. She shrugged. "That's me. The understanding ex who was the last to know."

He frowned, his dark eyes troubled. "You know that's not how it happened."

Crap. Son of a... She needed to stop this conversation now. Reliving the details of their breakup wasn't how she was going to spend the rest of her New Year's Eve. "Let's just forget it, okay, Isaac?" She raised her champagne glass in a toast. "We're here to celebrate Abby and Clay."

He clinked his glass against hers and gave her a grateful smile. After downing the rest of his drink, he got up and held out a hand. "Dance with me? For old time's sake?"

Was he serious?

He stared down at her with tenderness in his eyes, the same way he used to look at her. A dull ache formed in her chest.

Physically unable to say no, she took his hand and let him lead her out on the dance floor.

Isaac slipped his hands around her waist as Etta James's "At Last" started to play, and Yvette wished with all her heart that the ground would just open up and swallow her whole. It was the same song they'd danced to at their own wedding eleven years ago.

"I really do love you, you know," Isaac said.

The sad truth was she did know. But she didn't know what to do with that. "You just love someone else more."

"Differently," he corrected. "I love Jake differently."

She let out a huff of laughter. "Passionately, you mean."

He didn't deny it. He just held her closer and whispered, "I'm so sorry, Yvette. I hope one day you can stop hating me."

She pulled away from him, stared him in the eye, and shook her head. "I don't hate you. I just hate the situation. Maybe one day we can have a friendship again, but right now I need time to heal." Yvette leaned in and gave him a tender kiss on the cheek. "Be happy, Isaac."

Yvette walked away before he could respond and headed straight for the open bar. She hopped up on one of the stools and said, "Tequila. The good stuff."

"Rough wedding?" the bartender asked, already reaching for the Don Julio bottle.

"You have no idea." She gazed at the beautiful man in front of her. Damn, where had her sister found this one? Hotties R Us? He had the greenest eyes she'd ever seen, thick dark hair, and a five o'clock shadow that should've been illegal.

He set the shot in front of her and offered her a lime. She shook her head and downed the tequila. She grimaced and nodded for another.

"Was that the ex?" he asked, refilling her glass.

"Yep. The ex." She glanced over at him and practically growled when she spotted Jake. "And that's his new someone."

The bartender frowned, seemingly confused. "Are you talking about the man leaning in to—oh," he said when Jake planted a kiss on Isaac's lips. "Brutal."

She raised the tequila shot in the air and downed it. This time it went down nice and smooth. "The wife never sees it coming."

He raised one eyebrow. "Never? It was a complete shock?"

"Yep. We'd been having sex right up until the week before he split." Her face heated. She hadn't meant to blurt out her business, but apparently tequila gave her loose lips. "Oops. Probably TMI, huh?"

He chuckled, his eyes sparkling under the twinkle lights. "Don't worry about it. But maybe slow down on the tequila. You don't really want to get falling down drunk at your sister's wedding, do you?"

"As a matter of fact, I think I do." She grinned, feeling better than she had in weeks. "But because I love my sister, I'll try to keep it at just slightly drunk."

"Good plan." He winked at her, then moved down the bar to refill Wanda's wine glass.

"Whoa," Wanda said, in a too loud voice as she grabbed his biceps. "Where did you come from?"

He gave her a patient smile and said, "Southern California."

"Well, Mr. Southern California, do you have a girlfriend?"

"Not at the moment."

She raised her eyebrows. "Boyfriend?"

"Not my team," he said.

"Thank the gods for that," Yvette said.

He glanced over at her, that amused smile playing on his lips again.

Wanda glanced between them, then let out a tiny irritated huff. "Right then. Nice to meet you, Mr. California."

Yvette watched as Wanda wandered off back to the dance floor where she joined Hanna and Faith as the three of them danced with wild abandon.

"Well, Mr. California. Do you have a real name?" Yvette asked him.

"Mr. California has a nice ring to it." He nodded to her shot glass. "Refill?"

She shook her head. "I think I'm in the mood for something a little more... exciting."

"Like?"

Yvette swept her gaze over him, imagining what he'd look like with his shirt off. If his forearms were any indication, the man was built.

"I see," he said.

"Huh?" She glanced up to see him smirking at her. "Oh, damn." She laughed nervously. "Caught."

He held up a finger and said, "Wait here." Then he disappeared for a moment. When he returned, he was wearing a suit jacket and slipped out from behind the bar. He walked right up to her and leaned in. "Ready to go?"

"Where are we headed?"

"Anywhere you want to go, pretty lady. Anywhere you want."

Yvette stared up at him, shocked. Yes, she'd been practically drooling over him, had wondered what was under his button-down shirt, and might even have imagined what it would be like to be in his arms. But she'd never seriously considered spending the night with him.

He glanced across the venue at Isaac. "Look," he told her.

Yvette followed his gaze and saw Isaac staring right at them. His eyes were narrowed and his fists clenched. "He's jealous," she said, shaking her head. "Can you believe that? *He's* jealous."

"Exactly," Mr. Southern California said.

She glanced from Isaac to the bartender and back to Isaac again. Yes, it would be incredibly satisfying to walk off with the gorgeous specimen in front of her, if only she knew who he was. She stared up at him. "What's your name?"

"Jacob."

She let out a bark of laughter. "You can't be serious?"

"If it bothers you, you can call me whatever you like."

"Nope." She hopped off the stool, slipped her arm through his and said, "If the ex can have a Jake, I sure as hell can have a Jacob. Let's go."

They walked from the orchard to the parking lot in front of the Townsend home. Jacob gestured to a silver Mercedes. "That one's mine."

"Really? Bartenders must do really well these days," she teased.

"Something like that." With his hand on the small of her back, he led her to the passenger side and charmed her when he opened the door for her.

She didn't hesitate. She climbed in as if she hadn't just met this man thirty minutes ago.

He was in the driver's seat before she could even get her seatbelt buckled. Then they were flying down the road toward town. "Where do you live?"

"We're going to my place?" she asked.

He glanced at her, his expression amused. "Yes. Where did you think we were going?"

"Uh, I don't know. Are you staying at the inn?"

He shook his head and chuckled. "No, I'm not. I thought I was offering you a ride home. But if you had something else in mind..."

She stared at him, her mouth open. Then she shook her head. "That is not at all what you thought we were doing here. And you know it."

He glanced over at her, his expression heated as he let his gaze sweep over her again. "Is that what you want?"

"Yes." She'd made up her mind the moment she'd decided to leave with him. One night of debauchery with a man she wasn't likely to ever see again was exactly what she needed.

"You got it." He accelerated, suddenly eager to get to their destination.

"Turn left at the next street," she said. Less than two minutes later, they were parked in front of her house.

He killed the engine and turned to her. "Are you sure about this?"

Yvette answered by climbing out of the car and gesturing for him to follow. A slow smile claimed her lips when she heard his footsteps behind her. He followed her so close she could smell his woodsy cologne. And while she was unlocking the door, his breath tickled her neck. She turned around, pressed one hand to his chest, and said, "I never do this."

"That's what they all say."

"Maybe." She worked his top button free. "But in my case, it's true. I've never had a one-night-stand before."

That smirk was back when he asked, "And you just assume I have?"

"Didn't you just imply this isn't your first go-round?"

He nodded. "Yes, I guess I did."

"Good. Then you'll have experience at this. My only request is that you make it worth my while."

He pressed both hands against her door, leaned in, and whispered, "Don't you worry about that, gorgeous. I plan to make love to you until the sun comes up."

She raised her eyebrows in disbelief. "You have that kind of stamina?"

"Take me inside and find out."

Laughing, she unlocked her door. "If you're as good a lover as you think you are, I'm in trouble."

"Damn straight you are," he said and followed her inside.

IT WAS JUST past eight in the morning when Yvette walked into her bookstore on Monday. She had a smile on her face and a bounce in her step that she hadn't had in weeks. Her night with Jacob had been exactly what the doctor ordered. She'd woken relaxed, sated, and completely satisfied.

And alone, thank the gods. She wasn't sure she could face him after the things they'd done together. She felt herself blushing just thinking about him and what she'd let him do to her.

"Good morning," she called to Dannika, her assistant.

"Oh, Yvette, there you are," Dannika said, abandoning the shelf she was straightening. "He's here."

"Who's here?" she asked, heading toward the espresso machine behind the checkout counter.

"The new investor. You're supposed to be meeting him this morning. He's waiting in your office."

"Oh, crap!" She'd completely forgotten. Thanks to Isaac, the impending divorce, and the division of assets, Yvette had been forced to take on an investor. She'd gotten lucky when Miss Maple had mentioned her nephew was moving to town and might be interested. In no time, the paperwork had been signed, and today was the day she was to meet her silent partner. It wasn't ideal, but it would allow her to keep her store and her income.

She pasted a smile on and strode down the hall to her office. She could hear someone talking on the phone, laying out plans for a redesign, new book stock, and a café. She pressed her ear to the door and had to stifle a gasp when he said, "It's quaint, but Hollow Books is a hobby store. By the time I'm done with it, it'll be a paranormal destination spot. That's right, all new everything."

"Excuse me," Yvette said, barging in. "The paperwork says *silent* partner."

"You might want to check the paperwork," the man said as he turned his head to greet her.

"Jacob?" she said.

"What are you doing here?" they both said at the same time.

Then Jacob spoke into the phone. "I've got to go. I'll call you back."

"*You're* my new investor?" Yvette placed her fists on her hips, her face burning with utter embarrassment. *Please, God, don't let me have slept with my new business partner.* It wasn't possible, was it? *Please don't let it be possible.* "You're a bartender."

He shook his head. "I was helping out a friend."

"The paperwork said Michael J. Burton."

He cleared his throat. "The J stands for Jacob. We call my father Michael." Jacob got up out of the chair, his face just as red as hers. "You never told me your name last night."

"You never asked," she shot back.

"I was a little distracted." He swept his gaze over the length of her body then shook his head as if trying to wipe the image from his mind.

"Oh, hell," she said as she slumped against the wall. What had she done?

DEANNA'S BOOK LIST

Pyper Rayne Novels:
Spirits, Stilettos, and a Silver Bustier
Spirits, Rock Stars, and a Midnight Chocolate Bar
Spirits, Beignets, and a Bayou Biker Gang
Spirits, Diamonds, and a Drive-thru Daiquiri Stand

Jade Calhoun Novels:
Haunted on Bourbon Street
Witches of Bourbon Street
Demons of Bourbon Street
Angels of Bourbon Street
Shadows of Bourbon Street
Incubus of Bourbon Street
Bewitched on Bourbon Street
Hexed on Bourbon Street

Last Witch Standing Novels:
Soulless at Sunset

Crescent City Fae Novels:
Influential Magic
Irresistible Magic
Intoxicating Magic

Witches of Keating Hollow Novels:
Soul of the Witch
Heart of the Witch
Spirit of the Witch

Witch Island Brides:
The Vampire's Last Dance
The Wolf's New Year Bride
The Warlock's Enchanted Kiss

Destiny Novels:
Defining Destiny
Accepting Fate

ABOUT THE AUTHOR

New York Times and USA Today bestselling author, Deanna Chase, is a native Californian, transplanted to the slower paced lifestyle of southeastern Louisiana. When she isn't writing, she is often goofing off with her husband in New Orleans or playing with her two shih tzu dogs. For more information and updates on newest releases visit her website at deannachase.com.

Made in United States
North Haven, CT
31 August 2023

40968006R00146